Blood Moon Rising

Anthology

By Filidh Publishing Authors

Foreword

On September 17, 1985, five men (Wayne Cook, Don MacIvor, Roy Salonin, John Spencer, and Grant Sullivan) sat around a kitchen table and decided it was time to meet the challenge posed by the Vancouver Island AIDS epidemic. These five men saw the growing need for accurate and up-to-date information and services relating to HIV/AIDS. That evening saw the birth of AIDS Vancouver Island (AVI), with the founders forming the first Board of Directors.

More than thirty years later, AVI now has offices in the communities of Greater Victoria, Nanaimo, the Comox Valley, and Campbell River. Our catchment area includes all of the Gulf Islands. We provide harm reduction based, sex-positive information, education, support, and a range of services that include nutrition programs, jail outreach, peer education programs, testing and treatment, harm reduction supplies and overdose prevention rooms, support groups and counselling, referrals, and so much more. We take evidence-based action to prevent infection, provide support, and reduce stigma.

We dream of a world free of HIV and hepatitis C. Until that time, those most at risk in our communities continue to be marginalized — not only by their disease, but also by stigma and discrimination, poverty, and despair. As AVI fights these diseases, we join with those we serve to provide services based on consideration and respect and to provide those affected with visibility and a voice in the community.

For more information, please go to www.avi.org or call us toll-free at 1-800-665-2437.

Hermione Jefferis
Manager of Health Promotion and Community Development
AIDS Vancouver Island

This book is a collection of short stories and poetry with a theme of recovery and redemption, dedicated to those who rise above the situations in which they find themselves to become inspiring survivors.

Table of Contents

A.B. King

A.B. King was born in a land without time and where it still doesn't exist … a great, empty flat land… the Steppes of Canada. No, time does not exist there. Only seasons do.

His entry into this timeless land was wrapped in a great, warm blanket of innocence. But that changed fairly quickly. He became a toddler, a child, a teen. All those passed. He was once a man. It took a long time, but he got over that stage as well. Eventually, he became an old fart who once thought he had something to say. It was as if he thought he had gained some insights into Life and gotten some Wisdom out of it. He outgrew that, too.

Now he just rambles on, prattling in the senility that he calls his Third Childhood—the Addled Age, Shakespeare's seventh age of man. After a life of adventures and living in "interesting" times and places, he looks forward to soiling his diapers and drooling in the peaceful mind-emptiness of degeneration… innocent once more… and to that next big adventure. For what dreams may that bring?

Mr. King's short story *Fuzzy* was published in *The Unvalentine Anthology* (Filidh 2015).

A.B. King offers up his newest published work, *Chasing the Dream*, with heartfelt appreciation to S.M.K. for her edits, sage advice, and long-distance email slaps upside his head.

Chasing the Dream

I'm an olde man sittin'

Or just lyin' abed.

Got flies in my kitchen,

Got flies in my head.

The flies in the kitchen I can swat. It's the flies in the head that bother me. Things I've done, things I've said, books I've read, and lies I've heard. The places I've been and things I've seen. The bones ache, the joints creak, the bowels ain't regular, and my attitude stinks.

I've been sitting on the front porch thinking about things that were. About how I'm not half the man I was and my better days are behind me. I'm not dead by a long shot, and I wonder what I will be. Too old to do much, yet too young to die. The energy is gone, and the stamina left with it. Wish I could do more than watch the grass grow.

Oh, I do the usual day-to-day survival things like chop wood for next winter's heat. I re-shingled my roof last summer, and I repair people's cars. I fix their plumbing and their computers. I design additions to their homes and mend their boats. I listen to their problems and offer sage advice. I play with their children, feed their cats, and snarl back at their dogs.

My son asked me when I was going to slow down, told me that I do more in a day than most folks do in a week. I said something about "if I don't do it, then it won't get done." I didn't tell him the greater truth at the time. I didn't tell him because I didn't know it myself.

I used to think that I liked helping people. I used to think that knowledge, once gained, should be freely shared. I used to think that experience should be told and used as an example so others don't go through the same painful experiences. I used to think a lot of things. Now I try not to think too much.

I used to do a lot of things, too. I used to be a child, a young man, a soldier, an architectural draughtsman, a cartographer, a printer, a graphic artist, and an entrepreneur. I was a reader and figuratively devoured libraries. And a dreamer: I built things that came from my mind, from boats to cars to houses. I played with aerodynamics and musical instruments. I shovelled mountains of cow shit on dairy farms and supped with the well-to-do and influential. I've travelled, and I've seen wonders. I've seen people being born, and I've seen people die. I've been a wage slave and an enlightened employer. I was a good husband and a better father. I've been to the mountaintop of elation and the abyssal depths of utter despair.

Days are long and need filling. One needs only so much sleep. After work, there is still time to explore and find out what one can do. Yup. There's much time in a day. Too much to idly waste. You can kill only so much of it before it kills you.

So, the awful truth of the affair is that I now know why I do these things that I do. I do them because I know how to do them. I do them so that I have something to do. I do them because I don't know what to do next. I've pretty much seen it all. I guess I'm just putting in time until the day I don't have to swat the flies in my head

Ach. Flies. Some days are full of them. This cusp of a New Year is no different from any other, so far.

Yup, the eve of another new year. I hope things will be different this coming year.

I said hope, not pray. (I am a realist, of sorts.) If there was a deity, some entity that took responsibility for its actions, that deity would have shown up a long time ago.

But I've been over that ground before, too. So, what's new? Nothing. Especially not me. Still looking for the flame of hope among the hope-less.

At one high-stress job in my much younger years, we used to go out after work for a few drinks. It was a socially acceptable way of unwinding. After a few years, the few drinks became many drinks. And talk. Always shop talk. One evening I got a little pissed off. After a 14 -hour shift on the heels of eight years of the same thing, I was getting tired. Tired of the same bullshit. And then talking about it over drinks. "Goddammit," I said. "All we do is work. And then all we do is talk about work. There is more to talk about than work. There is more to life than that." Stunned faces looked back at me as if I had just committed the ultimate heresy. A deadly silence ensued. I looked them all square in the eye and then shook my head. I stood up and turned to go. As I left, I heard the conversation return to work. They are probably still at it if they have livers. Nothing changes.

Anyway, New Year's Eve. This old rock has rolled around the sun on a trip of some 584 million miles. We went all the way around, only to wind up pretty much where we started. That hasn't changed one iota in the seven decades that I have infested this planet. Nothing else has changed either. Same old, same old. In a universe where the only thing that is constant is change, somehow humanity as a whole has managed to resist doing just that.

There are many mysteries in the universe, but none as unexplored as the human mind and spirit. It is unsettling, even terrifying at times, to go down uncharted waters. But it can be one heck of a lot of fun as well. There are surprises and joys. The inner voyage is the only one that matters. It leads to a better view of the outside. After a lifetime of weird happenings, I have come to accept that "there are more things in heaven and earth than are dreamt of in your philosophy, Horatio." There are channels, sub-channels, and connections that escape our awareness as we go in search of our daily bread.

I have a tendency to believe in dreams. Most are indeed the dumping ground of the mind. A clearing out of temporary files. But some are different. Those ones, I believe, are connections to a deeper level of ourselves. Connections to things even deeper than ourselves. Well beyond the Jungian collective unconscious. Some are allegorical or metaphorical. A few are a lot more than that. Now, I'll admit to the possibility that, due to my PTSD, with my neuro-transmitters running in ultra-mode, my dreams are nothing out of the ordinary. It is just my system that gives them a deeper, more vivid impact. It is equally possible that, due to my experience, I am just more in tune with what is an unseen reality.

Other people have postulated that. I deny any responsibility. My ego won't let me go there. Indeed, one wise man once said to me: "With you, I detect no ego." Neat. In my search for 'truth, wisdom, and pure thought,' that tickles my ego.

But I digress. Back to dreamland.

I am going to tell you about a dream. Oops, sorry folks, a change of plans. I am going to tell you about two. Oh, no. Make that two-and-a-bit. See? The Universe is constantly changing. I'd better get to the matter at hand before it changes my mind again.

The first dream occurred when I was about two years old. I cannot pin it down any closer. The only clues I have are: it was winter, and my mother told me years later that it was when she was sick while pregnant with my sister. Apparently, it was a bit of a tough pregnancy. My parents took a winter holiday to Texas to visit my snowbird grandparents, taking my older brother with them. I was too ill to travel with them, so I was left in the care of the town doctor and his wife. I haven't been back since, yet I have memories of their house. I could draw a fairly accurate floor plan, even today. I inherited my mother's astounding long-term memory. Just don't ask me where I put my coffee cup two minutes ago.

Anyway, to the "dream." It was daytime. I was on foot, climbing a hill. The ground wasn't like anything I had seen before. It was sort of a rusty red in colour, made up of smallish flat rocks. Totally unlike the dark brown, almost black, prairie soil that I knew. As I climbed the hill, I could

12

see a plant on top of the hill. It sort of looked like a tree, but not quite. It was taller than me, and the trunk was very thick for its height. There was only one branch. A thick branch, as thick as the trunk. It was about one-half of the way up the trunk. It shot straight out to the left, and then it shot straight up. This tree didn't have any leaves and was green in colour. Weird.

I reached the top of the hill and was standing a few paces to the right of the tree. I looked down the hill, in the direction I had been heading. A fair distance away, at the bottom of the hill, I saw a car. There was a man there. He was pointing something up at me, or at the tree. A boy was standing to the man's left. He was looking upward, too. I recognised my older brother. I jumped up and down, waving my arms and yelling his name to get his attention. Neither my brother nor my father seemed to see me. I was bitterly disappointed. That is about all I remember of that dream.

I've told you about this dream because of what happened about ten years later.

One evening at home, Dad was showing home movies. One was their trip down to Texas. It was the scene I have just described. From their viewpoint. Without me in it.
Excitedly I said, "I remember that. I was there." Dad said, "No. You weren't. Stop making things up. Stop lying."

Fuck him. I was there. Beside that cactus.

No one can make me believe anything different.

Soren Kierkegaard wrote, "The self is only that which is in the process of becoming." My process continues with dream number two. You may place your own value judgements on it. I will not be there to argue in defence.

My sister knows of this dream. So does one other person. That makes you number three. A very select club.

When I was younger, much younger, I had a dream. When I awoke, I couldn't remember it. But as I aged, I had other dreams. 'Searching' dreams. Somehow I was trying to return to that particular dream. To a place in that dream. Somehow it had imprinted itself on me despite being another one of those things that disappeared into a black hole.

The searching dreams would start off with me travelling down a road. I would approach some dwellings. Over the years of the dream's re-occurrence, more buildings appeared in this settlement. Eventually, the road itself changed. As it got to this village, the road veered off to the right. North.

Eventually, the road became paved, and the village itself was accessible only by a service road. An old gas station sat at one end. This was a puzzling new addition to the dreams. I knew that something, a path maybe, lay behind it. But the searching dream took me away, down the paved road. I would awaken feeling a journey had been left unfulfilled.

Over the years, the pull of that dream became stronger.

One year, my right foot suffered a severe injury, and I could poke three fingers all the way through. After several surgeries, I spent three months cleaning and dressing the wound as it closed on its own. During this time, the pull of The Dream became irresistible. I had to revisit it. I had to feel it as if it was the first time, not a repetition. I needed the original. Not a remembrance.

It had been rainy and cool of late. I had cleaned the carpets, throwing more moisture into already burdened air. To help the carpets, the air, and me dry out, I had had fires in that place where one has fires when one is indoors. Calm, soothing, gentle, organically fueled warmth. Most pleasant with a book and cup of hot chocolate.

It was a beautiful evening outside. Night, actually. 14 degrees Celsius. Dewpoint 13C and 82% humidity. Slightly foggy. The air seemed thick. A sound-deadening type of thick. Man-made noises were muffled, but natural sounds, such as crickets, were surprisingly crystal clear, almost accentuated. Then... silence.

Blessed silence.

There is a lot to be said for silence. How's that for an oxymoron?

It was one of those nice, calm times. A good space, when the air is so sweet and, in spite of the low temperature and humidity, it is warm—as if the night reached out and wrapped you in its arms with a big gentle hug.

(*sigh*)

Ah, back to the hot chocolate and the fireside and the pull of the unknown.

Cloaked in the warmth of the night and the fire, and embracing a rising sense of adventure, I said, "Okay. Let's go there." I sat down to meditate. I started the relaxation exercise. I slowly closed my eyes. I started the breathing patterns. But instead of reaching for mind-emptiness, I focused on the dream. It was an abuse of the meditative process, but it was the only tool I had to put me in the right frame of mind.

The dream answered my call.

I was driving. I crested a hill and started down the slope. I could see the village. I could see the paved road veer off to the north. Instead of following that road as I had so many times before, I went into the service station parking lot and stopped. I got out and looked around. I headed around to the back of the station. I knew something had to be there. I had to find it. I looked at the tall trees and the thick underbrush. There it was. After all these years. An old overgrown vehicle path. I walked down it. And down it. And down it. Going west. The undergrowth thinned, and the path became a nice country road bordered by tall black spruce.

Suddenly, the road ended. Severed by a sheer-sided chasm. A river roared far below. Looking to the left, it went on and on. Looking to the right, it went on and on. There was no way down or up the other side. There was no way around it. No going over it. I was stopped. I knew that what I was looking for was somewhere on the other side. And I had to get there. This was a barrier that had to be crossed. There had to be a way.

In my mind came the thought: confession.

I must confess to what I had become.

Then I could cross over. Continue.

What I confessed is between me and me. Suffice to say, I was honest.

In my head came the words: "Here, you may not do that." And I was abruptly on the other side of the chasm.

I walked down a well-worn footpath. I found dwellings made out of animal skins, all in a forest of black spruce. No undergrowth. But there was also no people.

I approached a dwelling. In front of it was a tripod made of sticks. They were tied together about three-quarters of the way up, forming a nest. Cradled in that nest was a beautiful coloured globe. Mainly blue. A pattern moved, ever-changing, over its surface. It glowed as if lit by internal light.

I was drawn inexorably to it. As if it wanted me to take it. I picked it up and turned it over in my hand, looking it over. Admiring it. I put it back. It's not mine, I thought. I then noticed an older, wizened man sitting cross-legged in front of his doorway. He looked at me knowingly.

"It's beautiful," I said.

He nodded.

"May I take it with me to the Edge?" I asked. The Edge was a slot between trees, on a cliff overlooking a glorious valley. Surrounded by mountains. How I knew it, I don't know. I just knew. It was a place of contemplation and meditation.

"Yes, but don't lose it," he replied.

And so, off I went.

In the dream, I fell asleep. I awoke. The globe was missing. I searched in panic for it. It was gone. With a heavy heart, I went back to the village. I went to the old man.
"Where is the globe?" he asked.

I started to make excuses and stopped myself. "I cannot lie," I said. "I lost it."

He reached into his garment. He smiled and said, "It's okay. It knows where to go," as he put it on its stand.

I was shown to a dwelling and told I could rest there. I must have fallen asleep again because the next thing I remember is hearing a drumming and singing. I went to the door and moved the skin aside. It was dark. There was a fire.

People were drumming. Dancing and singing. I was dressed as they were. I went out and joined them. I sat down at a drum picked up a padded stick and started drumming in unison with them. And singing. Chanting.

The smoke from the fire rose, then spread out like a cloud layer. It was if there was a ceiling. The layer started to sink. And I started to rise. My head entered the layer. My head penetrated the layer. My head entered another dwelling. But no other part of my body emerged. Just this head sitting on the ground. The drumming and chanting continuing below me.

Above the layer, Old wizened men sat. I was facing the eldest. They were talking in a language that I did not know but understood. A ceremony was taking place. The tests of honesty and truthfulness had been passed. I was being welcomed into their family. I was given a name. My tongue cannot bend itself to make the sound, but I Know the meaning, the translation.

The ceremony above over, the celebration below continued.

I was standing to the right of an elder. It was still dark. We were alone, facing East on the edge of an apparent cliff. An abyss at the edge of their realm. Somewhere over the dark, misty distances came the faint, but persistent howl of humanity's pain, anguish, and suffering. It pierced my soul. I turned my head to him. He was taller than me. I asked: "What can we do? There must be something we can do. Something, anything to ease the suffering."

"We Chant," he said, with a deep, thoughtful, almost sorrowful look on his otherwise calm face.

I was bitterly disappointed. I thought something more immediate should be done. Something, like get involved.

We turned to return to the village.

I woke from my meditative state at that point. I was elated. Energized. Have you ever had an excited tickle in your stomach? The kind you get when something wondrous happens to you? Then you know what I am talking about. It lasted for weeks. It lasted so long; it was getting painful.

I could get into a lot of sidebars at this point. But I am not going to. I am going to let it be. As it is. For what it is. I know what it means to me.

I haven't tried to go back since. If I could, I would like to return to that place. After all these years, after all these experiences. To stand with that Elder Brother, where we stood. And I would turn to him and say: "I see your point."

There is no way that we can drop into that maelstrom of conflicting energies, appetites, desires of the modern world and hope that we can change things. We cannot introduce our presence in the hope of creating some peace and contentment. We cannot instill a calm equanimity and expect it to be maintained in the apparent conflict of daily life. Dreadful things happen to watchers and observers who try to become doers. One may not interfere in another's process. One may only stand by and render such assistance as is possible under the circumstances, should it be asked for.

Karma has a way of driving that point home. Paybacks are nothing. Blowbacks are a bitch.

Yes, the only way we can hope to alter things is to Chant. And to live life as an example of what we believe, of what we have become, of what we are. And hope the vibrations of the Chant have a ripple effect. All other action is doomed to failure. At great personal cost. After all these years, I see that. I now understand that sorrowful, faraway look upon the Elder's countenance. And so this New Year's Eve, like every other new day's eve, I Chant.

Dreams can hold a mirror to our faces and change our lives if we let them.

As was written in The Iliad, "for a dream too, comes from Zeus."

The Chant comes from within.

Thank you, Zeus. Thank you for ALL the dreams.

Hey, Zeus. While I have your attention, can you please do something about the damned flies? After all, Odin did say he'd put an end to ice giants. Just sayin'...

Astra Crompton

Astra Crompton is an artist, author, and creator based in Victoria, Canada. She uses several mediums to bring her visions and worlds to life, including illustrations, comics, short stories, murder mysteries, and novels. She has published two novels, a book of short stories, and four comic volumes. Astra's two short stories, *Dumpster Gardens* and *The Shore*, are featured in the *Anthology for a Green Planet* (Filidh 2014). You can follow her work at https://www.astracrompton.com, on Facebook @Astra Crompton, and on Twitter @ulzaorith.

Catharsis
A Primal Crusades story

Jasper Weisspapir was different. He was a Shifter. A Were-Beast. Most Shifters were mammals, but there were a fair few birds, the occasional reptile. It wasn't hereditary or cellular. It was just a facet of the soul for a tiny percentage of humankind. The moon didn't cause the shift. The transition was a matter of will or of stress, and Shifters had to learn to control it. Still, the full moon brought out their primal sides and was usually what outed what you were to others in the community. Other Shifters tended to notice the telling signs because they felt the pull too. That or their heightened senses could smell the beast in you.

The full moon had a different effect on each of them. Sure, there were some compelled to howl, but the heart of the change was passion. For one night a month, that passion overtook you, senseless and wild, wholly consuming. Jasper had friends whose hearing became so acute they needed to hide away from the world until it passed, others who needed hours of sex and it didn't matter with whom.

For Jasper, it was art. He went into a sort of trance, had to create, didn't matter what with. In his teenage years, he'd snatched whatever household objects were at hand: condiments, toilet paper, old magazines, even shredded a couch throw once. He'd woken up each morning after to find the nearest wall or floor plastered with a several-feet-wide creation. They were visceral, textured, and raw. They conveyed emotion, whatever had been going through his mind in the waxing days. And they were far more skilled than anything he could create on his own when 'Moon Sober'.

His mother didn't understand, of course. She didn't know he was a Shifter. She thought her son was—at best—on the autistic spectrum, some sort of savant. At worst, she was convinced he was in with a bad crowd and high on something. She never dreamed that ever since her son had turned 14, Jasper could turn into a skunk.

A fucking skunk.

Not sleek and glamorous like Lee's white sable. Not cool and casual like Adelaide's calico house cat. Of course, in the Shifter community, the jokes abounded. Shifters liked to ask what you were, and many wore their beast with an air of pride. Jasper hated admitting his form because everyone had to comment. Some said he ought to talk in an outrageous French accent and be obsessed with "finding love". Less kindly others would quip when he came into the room, what's that smell? Cue generic laughter and Jasper's well-trained obligatory smile.

Then college came. He got into comics, started drawing for the college paper about his queer experiences in a strip called LogOff. It wasn't autobiographical. His persona, Jared, was much cooler than Jasper himself. More confident, more brazen about his sexuality. Jared was also not the protagonist, but the chummy side-kick to a straight man living with queer friends. People in the pride club said he really spoke to them. That his humour helped them relax about concepts of gender. It was nice to hear, but really, it was just a strip comic with a weekly gag. He didn't have any lofty ideals.

It turned out that The Circle—the university's pride club—was full of folks like him. Not just queer, but

Shifters. There were even a few regular old humans who were friendly to their second-natures. It felt good to be able to talk about things openly, to be honest about what was going on in their lives. There was a lot to process: first puberty, then the fact that there was this whole secret layer of the world where folks turned into animals, and then trying to navigate budding gen der and sexuality on top of it. If it hadn't been for the friends he made there, he likely would have become a hermit. Just gone to live in a cave somewhere where no one would comment on his idiosyncrasies, and perhaps in four thousand years archaeologists would find his monthly paintings and wax prosaic on the messages left by an ancient people.

Outside of the club, he had classes, classmates, professors—all faces in a bustling crowd of strangers.

That was around the time he first met Lee McClaire, the white sable. He was the one face that stood out, attracting Jasper irresistibly. And, cliché as it sounds, that's when everything changed. For better and for much, much worse.

Lee was glamorous, beautiful, and brazen. His artfully cut hair was glossy black, but Jasper learned he fastidiously dyed it. His eyes were icy blue and permanently rimmed with smoky black eyeliner. His wardrobe was invariably white and impeccable. He wasn't afraid of showing skin, and among the masses of sun-bronzed jocks, Lee's porcelain complexion was like a beacon of hope for the gay kids trying to figure out how to just be.

Women loved him. Lee was known to sleep occasionally with one of his groupies, but he was incredibly picky. He had a sort of competitive harem where they'd jockey for attention, then preen if they managed to turn his head.

But as much as Lee liked a romp with a beautiful girl, he loved his men. He defined himself as "gay with aesthetic exceptions." Jasper once joked that Lee was too narcissistic to refrain from sharing himself around. Lee took it as a high compliment, regardless of the fact that it wasn't meant as one.

Still, with Lee as a poster-boy for overt pride and sexual confidence, it bolstered the quieter kids, straight and queer alike. His unapologetic shining helped everyone felt a little less weird about whatever they liked or wanted. Jasper was one of the crowd that watched and learned and eased into his own realisation. He had female friends, of course. He found he generally got along well with people, irrespective of gender. But what made his heart pound and his body heat up was men. And, as much as he hated himself for being one of the sheep, Lee was by far and away the most desirable man he knew.

Now, Jasper understood that he wasn't bad-looking. In fact, he could have been a romantic lead in a sort of Disney straight-to-DVD sequel. He was tall enough, fit enough. Hazel eyes that weren't quite green and weren't quite gold. Tousled ash blond hair that just misleadingly looked like he'd moussed and styled it. As the awkwardness of teenage transition fell away, he was reasonably happy with how his genetics had settled down.

But Lee had high standards. Exceedingly high standards. And no matter how generally pleasant Jasper's genetics were, there was nothing extraordinary about him.

Nothing Lee would want. He might have come up with stories about 'refining who he was' for his friends, but when he started piercing his ears and wearing eyeliner and nail polish and dying his hair silver... it was really all for Lee.

By some weird twist of fate, the makeover actually worked.

Lee first noticed him on the club dance floor. They danced, they kissed, they shagged in a bathroom stall. Jasper felt as high as if on the best Ecstasy he'd ever taken. He figured that was it, his one moment in Lee's fickle sunshine.

But somehow, it kept happening. Club floors, back of cars, dorm rooms... Until one day, Lee actually talked to him in class. Jasper could feel all of the eyes of Lee's little posse hone in on him. He felt suddenly like he had a target painted on his chest. He had a pang of fear that they would call him out for being a poser, a phoney with his painted nails and dyed hair. No one did. Lee asked him out. So they became a couple.

Lee's star-power catapulted Jasper into the limelight. All of a sudden people started paying attention to his comic strip; he started getting fan mail for it. Strangers would stop him in the halls and ask what he planned to do with the characters next. His friends in The Circle jeered at him, in a friendly way, about his new status on campus. He didn't see them less, but he felt like their conversations shifted somehow. Like, the group of friends that knew the real him forgot who that guy was, let him be superseded by this club kid who was allowed to escort Lee to class. Maybe it bothered Jasper a little, but he never said a thing.

Lee partied like a rockstar. He could handle himself. He knew his limits. He drank, did a lot of drugs. So Jasper joined him. Cocaine was Lee's favourite, and he especially liked to fuck while he had white flowing through him. He still got good grades (advertising and marketing) despite all the partying. They'd dine together, go to the movies arm-in-arm. And everywhere they went, people would turn to look at them. Lee had so much confidence that no one dared heckle. Jasper drank it all in, feigning confidence of his own, and praying that someday he'd feel that strength genuinely.

Now and then, Lee would let the act drop. His affected speech would simplify, suddenly articulate and be piercing in his observations. The act of Lee McClaire was a heightened, caricatured version of the real thing. Underneath all the glamour, he was insightful, focused, and demanding. He had almost no relationship with his family, and not for any dramatic reason or terrible coming-out montage. He just flatly stated that they weren't his people. He didn't belong there. They had seemed to sense it and had just let him get on with his life. End of story. Now and then he would jealously listen to Jasper on the phone with his mom, especially when Jasper was talking about life and school, convincing her that he was, in fact, fine.

Until one day when he wasn't.

Jasper's world stopped. All because of one little test. Not for his classes, but for his health scan. At some point, during all the clubbing, the trysts, the drug-fuelled hook-ups... Jasper had contracted HIV. This wasn't the 80s when the scourge was rampant throughout the gay community, but it was still an invisible marauder that could destroy immune systems and lives. It was still extremely virulent. There was still no cure. And now Jasper was infected.

Lee flipped. He screamed obscenities, he panicked, he refused to let Jasper touch him—Jasper who was a sobbing mess on the kitchen floor. And like that, Jasper's love for Lee fizzled out. This vain, arrogant boy was too pretty for the personality underneath. Lee cared for no one but himself. That was it; their relationship that had never been defined was over. Jasper was left to deal with this world-shattering news all on his own.

His friends from The Circle came to cheer him up. They tried and failed. They thought it was just a bad break-up. He didn't want them to know yet. Lee went back to his entourage, almost entirely unscathed. People said he was sharper, less gregarious than before. Some said he was mourning the loss of Jasper, but that only made Jasper angrier than ever. He hadn't been lost; he'd been fucking discarded.

His nail polish chipped, his eyeliner ran. His roots grew in, decidedly un-silver, and he just let them come. Eating became a chore. He was afraid. What did the disease mean for who he was? For the lifestyle he had so fully embraced?

In shame and fear, he drove three hours outside of town to visit a clinic where no one would recognise him. They did blood tests to check his CD4 count. He was prescribed some anti-HIV meds. He would need to have regular check-ups on his T-cell count. Because of his history with alcohol and drugs, he'd need liver tests as well. Punctured and woozy from watching his blood fill up the vials, Jasper couldn't help but feel that he deserved being a lab rat. Was this penance for all the heedless fun? Was this fate's way of telling him he had to grow up? Did growing up mean he'd never grow old, now?

He received no ready answers, just plenty of reassurance that he was otherwise healthy. That the medication—while it could have side-effects—had become very advanced. That he could live a normal life for years if he made smart decisions and minimised other complications and infections. He had never been an especially tidy person, and certainly not a fastidious one. Now, he would need to rethink how he kept his apartment. He'd need to be more cautious, and he'd definitely need to take better care of himself. On days where a bottle was oh so inviting, it was harder than it should have been not to drink. He never thought of himself as having an alcohol problem. Now he feared that perhaps his dependencies were more insidious than he'd supposed. Somehow, he associated the starving himself of alcohol as starving the disease. It helped.

He tried to head back to the club one night, on his own, just to find some release in dance. Many of the old friends didn't talk to him. He wasn't sure if Lee had said something, or if they didn't recognise him; his manner and style more quiet than before. The bartender, Chassidy, was the only one who greeted him by name. While there wasn't anything specifically said, she made his first drink on the house and kept offering to 'listen if he needed it'. He escaped to the bathroom with noncommittal responses left in his wake. Even the urinal seemed unknown, and he found himself irrationally afraid of touching anything lest he contract something—hepatitis, E. coli, tuberculosis! He turned around and left.

That was the last time he tried to pretend that his old life was still there. It had gone. It was not waiting for him to re-emerge. It was better just to concentrate on classes and go home alone at the end of the day. His apartment became his cocoon.

When the full moon came, he holed himself up in his room, dreading what emotions would be distilled into his monthly mural. His heart ached with disappointment. His dreams were reckless and exhausting. He was conscious of being afraid in ways he hadn't been since childhood. Suddenly dark alleyways sent his skin into prickles. An unknown face in a crowd that stared at him too long put him into a downward spiral of panic. He seemed to be trying to hide from the world, hide from everyone. He knew that he had changed. He had to live that every day. The last thing he wanted was for his artwork to show him just how much of a toll had been taken.

He woke to find his latest creation plastered on the wall above his bed, an intense black mass. It looked like cancer, like a vortex. It was made of acrylic paint and toner cartridge and pages torn from his statistics textbook and the tattered remains of his clubbing clothes. The mural seethed, angry and disturbingly hungry. He never named his pieces, but this one he named Catharsis.

And that was that. His old life was over. He shelved it, boxed it. Now he had to figure out who he was. No more hiding behind Ecstasy. No more losing himself on the dance floor. No more finding the man he wanted to be in the bottom of a glass. He changed majors twice. He lost some friends, made some new ones. Got back to drawing.

He found a doctor in town he could talk to, did some research. He could live with this disease. The changes he needed to make were not as scary or as drastic as he had initially thought. His body was reacting well to the medication. His T-cell count was high and healthy. There were no side-effects yet. He felt the first measurable degree of relief. His life was not, in fact, over.

He tried to have a few encounters, where he told men that he was positive upfront. Most of them lost interest. He understood their fear. The only difference was, he couldn't walk away from it as they could. Somehow his friends found out. They were suddenly gentler with him, conversations more hushed. It made him feel like a leper.

Sydney, the editor of the school paper, saw him recoiling again and took him aside. They had been friends since freshman year, and Jasper had always respected his straightforward practicality. Sydney squared his glasses and looked into Jasper's face as if seeing him more clearly than anyone ever had.

"You are still Jasper. Sure, changes have happened— that's life. If you get a scar, it doesn't change the way you think, your skills, what you're passionate about. If it affects your mobility, you rehabilitate."

Jasper couldn't order his thoughts to reply. He tried to pull away, but Sydney just clasped his shoulders tightly, as though resisting the urge to rattle some sense back into him. "Shake off this melancholy, man! You're young, you're capable, and you're surrounded by people who love you. Don't miss out on life just because the rules have changed. Relearn how to play and get back in the game."

Sydney's words sank in. Over the next few weeks, plain old human though Sydney was, he became a key player in Jasper's rehabilitation. There were many discussions late into the night, many pots of coffee shared, many shitty B-Movies scathingly shredded over a few beers.

For the next full moon, Jasper's friend Adelaide paid him to spend the night at her house. She set him up in the room with a bunch of art supplies. He left her with a phoenix-like explosion of yarn across the floor and up part of the wall. She tipped him a dizzying grand. His spirits clung to those threads of gold and red and yellow, creeping up the door frame, daring to reach towards the ceiling. There was a way to go yet, but hope was re-emerging. He felt proud that this truth had come from him.

Spring break hit, and he left for a week—just turned into his fuzzy skunk form and slunk around the city, finally exploring this inner animal he'd been ashamed of for years. He embraced it timidly at first, then accepted it wholeheartedly, and with that, accepted many things about himself that he'd been running from.

After the break was over, he came back in more ways than one. He was quieter, listened more. Each night he'd do his homework with Catharsis hanging over his head: a reminder. Shifting became an escape, a way to feel hidden, safe. He spent many nights sleeping in his skunk form. It was easier, somehow, to cast off his human skin. More fitting to be reduced to something wild.

When his hair had fully grown out to its natural ash blond, his nails were still unpainted, and his new clothes were simple and plain. Jasper Weisspapir could finally look in the mirror again. He wasn't sure what he saw there anymore. There was suppleness to the man in the reflection that he didn't recognise. Sharpness in the glance that seemed more feral. But Sydney had been right: these were still his genetics. He was still Jasper and nothing—no person, no disease—could change that. He knew this, but he still had some work to do in believing it.

As part of his healing, he drew a comic that had nothing to do with his LogOff characters or storyline. It was a cartoon skunk asking his reflection 'What can I do?' and the reflection responding 'Life stinks'. It lampooned his own thoughts and challenged them. The answer didn't fit the question, but it was a question that could never have a simple answer. The reflection was his, but of course didn't truly reflect the person in front of the mirror. The skunk complaining about its own self-perpetuated smell bespoke his own weakness of fixating on unavoidable problems in his life. Jasper was continuously picking at a scab and so preventing it from healing. Strangely, the strip helped him break through his funk and to repair his own sense of self.

Sydney printed it in the school paper. Jasper hadn't meant for something so personal to be seen, but by the end of the year, people were wearing t-shirts silkscreened with his comic. He had no idea who printed them up, but he heard a rumour that the proceeds were being donated to an AIDS charity. His enthusiasm for art rekindled, and he resumed his comic strip. He still got fan mail despite the loss of Lee's limelight.

Lee himself now existed on another planet. They never made eye-contact, they never spoke. He seemed thinner, less vibrant. Somehow that was satisfying. A mutual friend said that he'd had a breakdown over their breakup. That Lee's heart had been broken. Jasper wasn't sure if Lee had a heart to break, but he supposed it was good that his ex felt *something* over everything that had happened.

After all, they had been together for two years. No matter how they defined their feelings, they had experiences created together, memories forged, time shared. That shouldn't be so easily brushed aside or so quickly forgotten. Not even Lee could be that inhuman.

Life had to go on for both of them. Jasper accepted that.

He still had friends who were dear to him. He could still laugh at comedy routines. He felt more empathy for human plight than he once had. The disease had rendered him more sensitive, more human than ever before. He was still afraid of where it would lead him, still felt more comfortable being alone. But Jasper wasn't miserable. Life was okay. Not great. Jasper didn't know what great would look like for him, but it was strangely comforting to realise he had never known that. His lack of clarity about who he was and what he wanted had not changed. He didn't know what he wanted to do with his life. The idea of finishing his degree left him feeling strangely at a loss. Many of his classmates expressed similar feelings of anxiety. This was not an unreasonable response for a twenty-something-year-old starting out in the adult world. There was more to ponder now, more to keep in mind, but he was managing.

After all the chasing and all the running he had done, he had finally stopped. Now it was just him with himself.

He had learned how to just be.

Brianna Kempe

Brianna has been in love with words from a young age, an affair that grew even stronger once she fled from the Political Science classroom to the writing room in her freshman year of college. She holds a Bachelor of Creative Writing from Miami University.

Brianna writes when she can, balancing motherhood, working outside the home, volunteering, and the desire for a fun and fulfilling life. Ideas are always floating around in her head. Some form of a work-in-progress always keeps her on her mental toes and her fingertips from getting too soft. Her short story, *Leather Bound Love,* was featured in The Unvalentine Anthology (Filidh 2015).

Lilith's Devotion

*"And desert creatures will meet with hyenas,
    and goat-demons will call out to each other.
There also Liliths will settle,
    and find for themselves a resting place."*
Isaiah 34:14; International Standard Version

Morningstar had been a companion for some time before he spoke of the wonder of the tree. He raved that the forbidden fruit was sweet and succulent, that the fruit would ripen off the vine if I plucked it off the tree and held it for just one day. It would be difficult to wait so long, he warned me. Adam, once he saw it in our home, would beg me to share it with him. We would be amazed at the way the juice would spill from the fruit and quench all of our thirsts. All of our thirsts, he stressed, even the ones we did not yet recognise within ourselves.

I was intrigued, to say the least. There were plenty of other delicious things in the garden, but none with any depth of flavour to them. They satisfied a physical need, gave us energy. They tasted sweet, succulent, sour. But nothing hit my core with the satisfaction of the perfect bite. Food I knew nourished my body but lacked nourishment for my soul. When I mentioned a lack of spiritual sustenance to Adam, he suggested meditation under the tree, close to that which was most pure and strong. It would help to guide my thoughts and my prayers, he said. I took it as an answer to my unuttered question, silent permission to explore the mystery of the tree.

And so I went. I did meditate for a while. I focused on the roots, which became the waves of the sea that was a day's walk from the centre of the garden. The trunk was veined, each section sustaining its own set of branches, twisted among one another, creating a combined strength that would never have been matched by just one. The branches reached across the sky, filling my landscape with growth and greenery, each smaller branch just as healthy as its parent, with leaves and fruit populating every inch.

But one piece of fruit caught my eye, over and over, as I meditated on the tree from its roots to its smallest branches on a backdrop of azure. I stood, wanting to get a better view of it. Sitting on the bottom branch, just a tiptoes' stretch away from my outstretched fingertips, it started as a whisper and grew louder. Was it my name or a warning? Lilith or Loyalty? Perhaps if I touched it, I would be able to decipher what it was saying...

As my fingers grazed the skin, it fell into my hands, belonging there. I held it to my nose, wanting to absorb it without damaging its beauty. I was torn. It was a piece of perfection unlike any of the other foods I had found so far in the expansive garden where I was given free rein to eat anything and everything. Except this. I wanted to be loyal. I had but one rule to follow. I wanted to experience everything. I had but one limitation.

I cradled it in my hands, wanting to keep it from bruising, wanting to protect it, to pamper it, to cherish it. I twirled it gently, looking for any blemish, but found nothing.

I treated it the way I had been waiting for Adam to treat me since we were paired together: tenderly, compassionately, adoringly.

I carried it to the place I spent many afternoons alone, while Adam concerned himself with husbandry and neglected his wife. Rather than hiding it in shadows, I placed it in a bassinet made of leaves and straw, in direct sun. It deserved to continue knowing the radiance of the sky, even though I had taken it from its first home. I knew that I did not want to eat it. I wanted only to savour the radiance of it, to keep it near me. I would use it to reflect on what it meant to cherish, even if I had no experience being the object of the awe.

The next day, its perfume had invaded my shelter. The smell intoxicating, I worked to find the strength Morningstar said I would not be capable of. Proving him wrong or following His rules, I was not sure which was more important, but both took precedence over succumbing to my desires.

On the second day, it began to shrivel, but the smell was just as sweet. Rather than taking it back to the tree where I had never seen one fall, I kept it in its crib. On the third day, it had crumpled to a fraction of its size, and there was no give in it when I pinched it, hoping to feel the same spring in its flesh as I had gotten the first day. I raised it to my nose, and the sweetness was just as pure. My tongue slithered out of my mouth, curiosity taking over my reflexes despite my dedication to the literal edict I had been given. I still knew I would not eat of it. My tongue just wanted to taste it.

The sky turned dark, thunder roared, and the fruit stayed close to my face as I listened with consternation.

"You are to leave and never to return. You may take what you want, including your precious fig, more important to you than the partner I had given to you, more important than the job I had given to you, more important than the rule I had given to you. Because of your selfishness, I curse you. Your hands will touch much, but your heart will be hardened. Live in peace, but not with me." The words were loud and definite, though there was no evidence they were heard by any of the birds or creatures nearby.

I spoke aloud, fearful that if I spoke the words only in my heart, He would no longer listen.

"But, I didn't eat it. You can have it back, and I will take care of the sprout that might come of its seed. Yes, I hid what I had done, but I wanted to relish in the experience, the scent, the heft of the fruit. I liked the feeling of it, and I wanted nothing more than to be closer to You, to the piece of You I could touch. That's what the fig is, isn't it? A physical reminder of all that You are, the greatness and grandiosity of You, the ultimate understanding of what is good and what is evil. I wanted to know you more, but You want to keep us at a distance. Is that fair, if You love us as you say you do? Perhaps let me nurture a seedling, let me become more like You, taking care of something as You take care of us. I can find peace with that, with Your help."

The answering silence was louder than any voice could have been. I waited, longer than was necessary, hoping that perhaps, if He saw my remorse, He would change His mind and allow me to stay. He would understand that I should not be banished. The sun set on me as I waited for the response I would never get.

I thought about returning to the home that Adam and I had shared, wondering if there was anything that I wanted to take. I could think of nothing that would have done me any good. And so I picked the fig up from where I had dropped it at dusk as my hand's strength had vanished. It would serve as a reminder of my choice. I would live up to what I had offered, in order to have peace with myself. Perhaps if I paid penance long enough, I would be welcomed back. Perhaps if I cared enough, care would be granted to me again.

I kept to the outskirts of the garden for a season, loneliness my only companion, and a bitter one at that. Excommunication is a deep and powerful punishment... and though I knew the word "hate" and could understand it as a concept, I did not, could not, would not feel it for Him. Perhaps if I had deserved it, had I actually eaten the fig, moved beyond observing its beauty off of the tree and holding it for myself, then would I be able to have the deep and lingering anger the snake implied I should for Him?

Alas, all I had was regret. For listening to the serpent, for hiding my curiosity, for not pushing harder against the exile, for not sharing the catalyst of my actions, for enduring this alone. I did not want the snake beside me, but Morningstar had combated my loneliness before. Most of all, I regretted that I missed him more than I missed Adam.

I had enjoyed his company while I walked the garden. I appreciated his help in developing names for everything we came in contact with. He was gracious and kind, willing to let me speak my mind, occasionally asking me to explain or describe further what I meant. We saw each other as equals; I enjoyed our conversations immensely. Attentive and compassionate, he fulfilled a need for me that Adam had never even recognised.

Morningstar had slithered into my life at the right time, as I was bending down to gather a vegetable too ripe to eat, but that would provide my daily quota of seeds. I had called it a zucchini, but Adam said summer squash. With either name, we would both want it available the next year and gathering a few seeds would earn me a smile from Adam. I had hated that I wanted that reward so much. That desire for compassion left a void the perfect size for the serpent.

"Please do not be alarmed. I would like to talk with you since it seems that we could both use a friend." I had been struck more by this animal's understanding of my needs than by the fact that I understood him.

I had needed a friend, though I would never have made such a claim. Adam should have been enough for me. There was work to accomplish, tasks to complete. There was inventory to take, language catalogues to make. We had worked, not necessarily together, but at least in conjunction, and we had made the most of our gardens and our time. Eventually, our day of rest would come, and Adam would look at me and be ready to engage my mind rather than just my nimble fingers. I had told myself I could wait as long as necessary. I would tell myself this while waking to the sun, and while falling asleep to the moon. I would tell myself at breakfast as Adam and I parted for the day, and at supper when we itemised our accomplishments.

Once there was someone else ready to acknowledge my needs, my patience had worn out. I had no longer wanted to wait for Adam to understand that my needs went beyond sowing and harvesting the literal produce of my work.

I had accepted the snake as my comrade, never questioning his motive in meeting my needs, and so

I was in full ownership of my benightedness and my choices. Free will was as much of a wrench as excommunication is, it seemed.

These memories haunted me as I wandered the outskirts of Eden, watching for any sign that I would be welcomed back in. The old fruit started to rot. As it did, I gathered the seeds that were inside. There were many, far more than I had thought possible from one small piece of fruit, and I wondered if that was the reason it was off limits. The number was more than I could fathom, and endless possibilities meant more paths to get lost on.

Rather than focus on the innumerable, I focused on two. One bag of many untracked seeds, to be made empty in time, and one bag of few, to add to as I counted seeds and days. As each dawn broke, I transferred one seed to the second pouch, trying to track how long I had been out in the nothingness.

Morningstar came by every once in a while, and we still spoke, though I was not as eager to engage with him. With each dawn, I told myself I was closer to being accepted back in. I would survive this punishment. Keeping conversation to a minimum made me suffer more, be more lonely, which I was confident was what He wanted from this time of exclusion.

Once he asked me what I had done with the fig and if I had broken down and finally tried it. I answered honestly that I had not, and that seemed to please him even more than it would have if I had said yes.

Occasionally, he asked what else I wanted to do, offering the idea of going in to sabotage something in the garden. Not yet, I told him, hoping that if I could last just another day, I would be granted salvation. But there was the "yet." Each day I found myself less faithful that my pardon would come.

Sometimes he shared tidbits about how Adam fared and what animals had been named. Morningstar told me about the appearance of another woman, Eve, and how she was far from interesting. She was not inclined to talk; she stayed attentive only to what Adam's instructions had been for the day.

The knowledge of Eve set the number of possible paths down to one. While I could imagine a loving family of three, I would not be seen as an equal after being evicted. Parity was important, and even with only Adam, I had never been granted that. With my tarnished record, her submission, and Adam's drive to fulfil only His wishes, I would never find peace in Eden. I worked to gather my courage as I planned to create as much distance between Eden and me as possible. It would take tenacity to journey from the only home I knew, further into a wild land that I could not be sure would provide anything for me.

Contemplating the journey ahead, I found an egg that had fallen from its nest, the embryo already consumed back into the circle of life. I gathered it, cleaned it, and filled it with dark soil. I chose one seed from the untracked pouch, and wondered if I would be able to nurture its growth, stunted as I was with anger.

I kept the soil moist, sometimes with my tears and sometimes from the river. For each day that passed, I found myself growing more certain that I should leave; He did not deserve forgiveness. He had punished me for wanting to know Him better. What kind of love did that exemplify? None, in my opinion.

Finally, a tiny sprout popped up through the soil, and I was rewarded for the patience I had given to this living thing. Growth and change had occurred, and I could take some credit for that. I had nourished it, rather than starved it. He had provided only famine for me, and I had shrivelled. With those first signs of green, I knew that it was time to leave where I was no longer welcome.

I knew I would carry on. Just as Eden would survive without me, I would survive without it. I did not need Adam; I did not need Him. I did not deserve the punishment I was facing, but I neither did I yearn for reconciliation. I had been told not to eat the fruit. I had not done that.

I carried only the pouches and the sprouted egg as I started to walk, not sure how far I could go, but knowing that I had to put space between me and what I had known. I fed on wild growth, sometimes abundant, often not, taking in far less than I thought I would have needed for the journey.

As I travelled, the sprout grew, taking over the shell. When it seemed as though it would crack its container open, I camped for a night, creating a sacred space for what I would leave behind. I removed it from the shell and planted it, not knowing if it would continue to flourish, but convinced I had done everything in my power to give it a chance.

In the morning I started out again, cultivating another beginning in the shell, no longer watering it with tears of anger and frustration; this time tears of sadness dampened the dirt. Loneliness settled into my bones, but I continued to walk, knowing that my muscles were not as weary as my heart. There was no cure for either.

I sowed countless seeds from the untracked pouch as I walked. Between the counter pouch and my trail of seedlings, I was on my last uncounted seed when I found the caves. Squeals echoed past me, starting low and ending piercingly. From a distance, I could make out the horns and beard of a creature I would never partner with. But despite the continued bleating, peace took over, and I was able to rest for the first time in what had felt like aeons, though the seasons had only cycled four times.

I wished that I could thank Him with an honest heart, but the words would have been tainted with bitterness, no matter how tired I was at this point. Exhaustion would never lighten the load of loathing. Instead, I rested, knowing that none of my tomorrows would offer the same chance again. There would be fruits to gather, paths to trod. There would be water to carry, a home to make. I had found a new base, and I could sleep deeply before the tasks of creating a home started, never to be completed.

When I woke the next morning, the bleating had ceased, and I could hear birds, their calls made with heavy hearts. Three sharp, clear, even pitches, followed by two descending tones. The end of the call reminded me of the sound I made when the sad memory of leaving entered my thoughts. I inched to the front of the caverns, listening intently and walking softly. I caught my first glimpse of the bird, hooded in black with a bright orange body. A beautifully sad song, vibrancy shrouded by a darkened mind. Kindred souls, we seemed to be.

I watched this bird longer than I should have, memorising the call, hoping that one day I might have the courage to call and she might respond to me. I watched, spellbound, until the hunger took over and I made myself pull away from the captivating melancholy that perfectly reflected my own feeling of persistent hope crushed by reality.

As I managed my survival needs, I thought back to the bird, wondering what shadows she carried in her own small beating heart. Were they as dark as mine, as deep and foreboding to the start of a new life? I had been banished from bliss, and as much as I recognised that Adam's paradise was not my own, it hurt to think back on my time there. It had been easier, even if just as lonely.

When I approached, animals scattered in all directions, able to recognise that I was a damaged being. They gave me space and time to myself, perhaps to tell me that I needed to focus on healing before I could be accepted. Pain was still the source of any and all adrenaline coursing through me. I depended on hurtful memories to spur me to the next new thing, to take on the challenge of living, just to prove that I could do this on my own. Alone. Without him. Without Him. The ache my only companion.

I worked from the pouch of seeds representing each dawn since expulsion, planting one directly in the ground each dawn. Not all survived without my tears and tenderness, but many of the trees grew strong and sturdy in this new land, though the fruit never came in. I considered destroying them, but the barren reminders were beautiful to me, and I always gave them one more cycle to come to fruition.

The loneliness was staggering, but so was the work to be done. I spent each sun's arc out in the land, gathering, tracking, and planning what would need to be done tomorrow. From dusk to the next light, I subsisted in those caves watching my orchard grow but not produce, wondering how much of a mirror it was to myself. I woke and rested in personal silence amidst hearing the bleating and whines, until my ears became numb to all but the call and cries of the birds. My heart stopped sighing the more I heard them. I was no longer alone. Something else knew my pain.

I had memorised the calls, with minor variances, and in time I found myself whistling a return. I could not remember the last time I had spoken, beyond knowing it must have been to Morningstar, but the need for communication won out over silence. In uncountable seasons, I got my first response, and my heart smiled more vibrantly than at any of those damning conversations I had once been so grateful for.

I trained hard, working to learn cadence and rhythm. When I was able to sing with the hooded bird, passing the melodies back and forth, my face and eyes smiled for what I was sure was the first time ever. My muscles and throat were raw at the end of that day, but the warmth of companionship helped to ease the aches. As I learned the chords of the other birds, I joined in with them more and more, and I was accepted into their chorus.

Smiles came more frequently, both in my heart and on my face, and I found that the animals in the area were more willing to be around me as my mood shifted. While I was never as comfortable around the wild creatures here as I had been there, I felt safe when a fox came near me. Even the hyenas' shrieks became less of an annoyance and more of a countered harmony. I was finding my way, on my own. Alone. But finally with some peace.

I sang a line back to one of the orange birds with the black heads, and as I did so, it flew down to perch on a branch near my hands, busy collecting berries for the next day's supplies. I had been accepted in their music. I had been granted rights to live among all of the animals, but never had any of them made it so clear that they also wanted to be near me. This one was choosing me, and I held my breath as I reached out to try to touch another living being. The bird shuddered a bit as my fingers stretched toward him. He hopped twice, in anticipation or fear, I was not able to tell.

I paused, wondering to myself if I deserved this connection. What had I done to make his world a better place in my time in these caverns? I had planted trees which bore no fruit. I had taken over potential shelter from the wolves and goats. I was taking some of the materials that would have been eaten by others and had not yet started a garden in order to replenish it all. I looked to the berries I was gathering and wondered aloud, expressing my thoughts as vocalised words for the first time I could remember since begging Morningstar to leave me alone after learning about Eve.

"What do I have to give?"

The bird did not fly away, but looked at me, the question burning deeper into my heart than even the first joy had at exchanging a song.

"A berry. I can offer a berry." I spoke softly, even a whisper difficult to form now that I was intent on speaking. Words had come easily enough when it was reactionary, but now that I wanted to be heard, I stuttered more than I would have liked. I picked the ripest berry I could find, plucked it off the vine, and held it in the palm of my hand, waiting to see if my offering would be accepted.

He moved to my fingers, and the tingling started as soon as his tail feathers brushed by fingertips, a physical connection with something else that breathed. I thought that perhaps I was just excited. As he nipped at the berry in my hand, the tingling moved from the tips to the fingers themselves, and the tips became numb. I could move them, but I no longer felt the feathers that I knew still touched my skin.

I tilted my head to the side, trying to get a better view of what else might be going on with the bird who was happily standing on my palm, eating a berry, letting the juice flow onto my skin. There was no feeling of malice in the bird's behaviour. The juice was a dark crimson and started to seep between my fingers as I realised I could no longer feel them, either.

Instinctively, I shook my hand, and I immediately regretted the loss of his small weight. I was struck by the absurdity that I had missed something I could not feel at the time it was lost.

He perched nearby again, and looked at me, a sense of concern flooding the small eyes.

"I'll survive; it was worth it," I promised him, and he chirped in relief. I chirped back, glad that we understood each other.

He was not the only one who would come closer to me, allowing me to get the touches that I realised I so desperately needed at that time. Dozens of their community would approach me, and so long as I could offer them something, a berry or an ant, for example, they would happily sit on my hand or my shoulder. In time, they would approach before I made an intended offering clear, but always I made sure that I had something to give them. I learned what they got excited about, what berries they loved to eat most, what insects made the least mess on my hand.

The sense of touch became less important to me, my hands becoming more calloused, now doing all of the work that Adam had, in building and creating a home. I did not notice the softness of the fruit as I once had in the garden. Nothing, I told myself, would ever compare to the fig, and so I no longer paid attention. I had no energy at the end of my day to focus on the texture of my own skin, and my hands were so drained from their tasks, I always wanted them to rest at the end of the day rather than exploring the sensation of fingertips tracing my body.

Each night, I lay down, crashing to sleep. Most nights I would dream of what I had done, what needed to be done. Never were there enough hours of darkness to delve into what I wanted to do. I reviewed the planting of the many seeds and the growing, if not blossoming orchard. I went through the harvesting and cataloguing everything this place had to offer, never feeling as though it had the expanse of Eden, but also never having a day when I did not find some new wonder, a flower or a fruit I had not seen before. No other fig tree outside of my orchard, but I occasionally dreamed of what I might do to get mine to start producing. Bringing rich soil to nourish them; bringing fresh water from the creek to refresh them. Always this had the lowest priority, as I realised on waking that the trees still offered me shade, offered the birds additional perches, and were a memorial to what was. That was enough.

One morning, before I was prepared for it, I found only one seed in the pouch, a bittersweet discovery. Lost in a new way, without my purpose of creating a possibility of new knowledge. So far, none had produced fruit, but with each seed there was hope. I could see Him choosing just one seed of a fruit to be ripe with growth. I wondered if Eve had won that contest, absolved from the concern that I would be responsible for raising young ones and feeling squandered with no such a task to accomplish.

That morning's planting ritual was either the most joyous or the most sorrowful. I could not decide which, and my emotions swept back and forth, encompassing the entire range. I held the seed with more care and compassion than I could recall giving to any since the first. I planted it close to the ritual I had performed the day before, using almost the same hole for the planting. I recalled the twisted trunk and the entwined growth of the original tree. I was not sure if I hoped it would take or not, both fearful of a stronger reminder of what I left behind and knowing that I would be grateful to answer my mind's questions of "what if" with "at least I tried."

I kneeled at the plot for some time, meditating on what I had been through, what I had learned and what I had given up. Abandonment, autonomy, allegiance.

This led to the realisation that I had been putting off starting a garden because the fig seeds needed to be tended. I thought over the tastes that I had experienced and decided that the sky-colored berries would be my first choice for cultivation. I stood, brushing the dirt off of my knees, and let one more tear fall to the small mound in front of me. I walked away, knowing I would come to spend more time at the altar of Self, but I did not look back that morning. My duty had been done, and it was time to move on. Instead, I went to explore the wild bushes nearby. There was gathering to take place, preparation of seeds to happen, a plot to choose. Tomorrow would come before I was ready for it.

I said goodbye to what had been, the expectations of a loving relationship with a man who was not grown enough to love me. I bid farewell to the possibility that I would ever want a loving relationship with Him, who had not seen enough potential in me to love me. And I welcomed what was to come, not an unquestioned devotion, but rather a devotion to questions. Who am I? What now? Why?

Janilee Porter-Hirsche

Janilee Porter-Hirsche has a Master's degree (MA) in Conflict Management and Prevention: Ethnic, Political and Security Issues. Her origins are United Kingdom colonist, and she strongly believes her ancestry is Celtic. She started life as a Canadian Army brat and as an adult has lived across Canada and on four other continents, always craving family, community, and roots. During a crucial time of necessary healing from a violent marriage, she was introduced to First Nations traditions. Under the personal direction of a Cree Elder who knew how painful her journey of healing would be, Janilee received essential spiritual guidance and rich experience beyond her conscious ability to connect or understand. Through this Elder, and through professionals connected with Women's Shelters and police services she released the illusions she had held dear, accepted the very painful truth of her past, and has moved forward as a survivor and witness.

Janilee is thankful to all her friends who cared; helped, emotionally supported, and encouraged her--especially her marvelous children. She is amazed by the indescribable mystery and power of connectedness. Janilee is currently an author, artist, and Bolivia Eco/Voluntourism Entrepreneur based in Bolivian Oasis, Tja Huasi, Bolivia. (bolivianoasis.com)

The Mormon Elder's Shadow

Struggling for breath and solid turf beneath the pounding tides of
His narrative
Sand. gasp. inky water. foamy.
surf. choke. sky. barnacles. scream. rocks. gulp. undertow. sun.
storm. frantic call. crushing waves. wheeze. bubbles. clutch lungs.   Brace!
Don't cry, don't give up. So close to shore--just there.
Wrong answer- wrong question. Desperate. Confused.
Bound by His narrative
My fault, my weakness

Tethered in a sea I love, forgive, respect, forgive, believe, forgive, trust and forever forgive
In shadow, I practice acquiescence, humility, compromise, subservience to His superiority His curiosities. (But if you love me, why this...)
He says He loves me--if only I didn't disappoint.
Bound by His narrative
My fault, my weakness

He gloats that others exult in His giftedness. Proof of His entitlement to use me
Dear wife He purrs, your feeble memory blocks what I bid when you are completely mine in that glorious 'Cock Drunk' state.
And He quivers with excitement in His telling, revealing, rejoicing, rehearsing, reciting the traumas, perversions, and dark secrets that please Him so. Briefly, He seems blissful, and He assures me He loves me.

Yet He challenges endlessly, never satisfied, one last test of
my love, one more game - never good enough. I keep
trying, and somehow I enter the abyss again
Bound by His narrative
My fault, my weakness

Shhh...

MASTER

Master
Of honeyed phrases
Of immaculate deception

Not a lie.
Fractured versions of truth
Manipulated, orchestrated
By a grand puppeteer, wizard, demigod

The brutality of provisional 'love'
Granted only through satiety of your hunger for
Darkly, starkly dehumanising deeds that tore my soul.
Why. Did. That. Make. You. Happy.

Yet, Master, we know that when you are happy, you
radiate such joy and intelligence
Exuding humility, generosity, and kindness
Spiritual leadership and love to the world.
You are brilliant my Master! I am blessed that you
persevere with me.
I stand by your side and smile waving to the crowd.
That many people can't be wrong.

And backstage the cycles continue as
Confused and desperate to understand
I wait and work to please and honour you.
I cleared the decks, so Master will be the wonderful
version
Unfettered by trifling chores and annoying
commonalities

Intrigued by sadistic curiosity
Master wonders how far he can push his treasured toy
Studied, experimented upon, used, abused
¨Shhh, shhh my cunt–never resist—'no' is not an option
Your Master is above reproach.

Confused by my Master's affirmations
My dear soul mate I love you but…
You are defective. You are wrong
I can fix you – trust me – I know exactly what God
created you for
My pet, my puppet, my whore, my slave

You exist at my pleasure--you will feel my wrath
If you dare protest your dignity or cease to appease me
No one will believe you my weary 'cock drunk' crone
In that day be gone, disappear – die¨
And the rich old white man will, of course, replace you
in a twinkling
The Master is above reproach.

Gaslit

Years of cycles no one saw, anticipated or
comprehended
Honeymoons and crises
I felt the blame; I accepted the responsibility
Forgave HIM for what HE needed to do
And then we started anew
And I tried and failed and tried and failed
Never enough, wearing down
Decade after decade
Seeking help to fix me for HIM
That which was not broken
My anxiety, my stress, my fault
HIS impunity
And then
HE found his younger version of me
Thank God because HE deserved no less.

He told me that with good luck he could have 20 years
of happiness
Finally.

Recent pharmaceutical crutches catastrophically altered
To attempt to slow my emotional decay under pressure
of HIS needs
While I tried to earn independent respect
Finishing a Masters' degree
Exhausted and now suddenly suicidal
Worth less
Worthless
Worth nothing
Convinced of HIS narrative.

Vicious sexual assault
Raped
By my Beloved
I deserved it because I was drunk
HE was stone cold sober
He is now disgusted by the older version of me
About to officially enter menopause
"No holds barred" HIS constant sexual prerogative
This night an extraordinary opportunity for HIM
To fully demonstrate to me my sole remaining soul
worth to HIM
A marathon of violent, pornographic sex
A pervert preacher
Brutalising his drunken, aging wife.

He began by categorising my body parts. Microlensed
HIS strawberry nipples on as yet firm breasts,
HIS shaved saucy cunt
HIS alabaster ass
All that HE ever cherished
And now HE could substitute the young smile HE
craved, the wide eyes HE anticipates
Photos before the punishing blows, chocking, bruising,
and tearing of
HIS old trash.

I was drunk (second time in decades) so it was my fault
HIS fingers twisted in my hair shoving my face onto
HIS cock
HIS burrowed fist pounding and ripping my swelling
cunt
Reaming my ass with gargantuan something
Slapping, hitting, glowering 'enough'?
On my back with my head hanging off the bed

HE standing ramming HIS cock down my throat
Gleefully suffocating me
Until HE was totally satisfied.

I reclined on one side off the bruises
And HE watched me take benzodiazepines, insulin, more
My extremities tingly, numbing, shutting down I thought, hoped, prayed
Somebody will ask why my body is so battered
My body will speak
My body will be my witness, testimony, final note
I am fulfilling HIS wish, my resignation.

Yet hell dawned with pain, shame, humiliation
HIS quiet smugness wrote in stone that
This too shall never be spoken of
No reason to forgive HIM
I knew it was my own fault
I deserved what HE did
As always HE was generously helping me become
More clear and confident in my worth
HE loved me despite the menopause.

****

Mere days later
When I could no longer hold myself above ground
And only grieve and wail utter failure
The woman psychiatrist offered me safety
And I crawled into her big protective arms
Relieved I could rest quietly
Believing she would
          Make HIM go away.

Surreal indivisible vignettes:
Same nurse again still always
Can't be. Different name
Compassion. Long hair pretty
Characters in books I know
I knew but cannot recognise
          Did I read or live this?

My LIFE partner enforced and reinforced
This is 'the menopause'
That's what happened HE said
Of course, I should want death
Useless to HIM now
          Blushing replacement in HIS sigh.

Confusion and restless paranoia
Dark meals aside cloudless August windows
Lights shifting. Bright. Black.
Spotlight beamed in on us
Every time someone spoke to me
          Crucial to signal something urgent
          From here inside 'the menopause'.

My psych ward roommate gifted me
A head of garlic. To protect me
She said she knew I needed it
She argued with unseen entities
To leave me alone while I slept or
Listened for my own breathing
Between buzzing sounds startling twangs
In my own head
          How have others survived 'the menopause'?

The nurse warns that I have a difficult reputation
Because my dear SPOUSE complains
Through the phone to 'The Nurses' Station'
I cry and harder, lost as a patient steadies me
'Don't worry dear, they will sort your meds out'
          For 'the menopause'!?

Vaguely ruffling somewhere
          Sudden antidepressants
I'm sick and tiring anyway HE said
Anxiety cocktail
Among the other prescriptions.

Other patients study fixate on
The great doors 'The Nurses' Station' controls
Anxious to escape, breathe summer's chlorophyll
Or sadly thirsting for Mom to finally arrive
          Did I beg my woman doc
          To take me outside to the trees
A cat and curled around her
With my arms and head too snuggly
Purring?

Now a skulking wolf prowling the barren corridor
Menacing 'The Nurses' Station'
Fortress of glass and high barriers and video screens
Back and forth watching them watching me
Noting observing their caged charges
Back and forth anxious path
          Do NOT cry
I smack the upper double door frame with my hand
As I pace – challenging fear.

Twitchy monkey me!
Caught by lit unlit little red lights
Seven tiny lines coding digits
Urging sequential increase – wow
sixtwofivefivefourfivefivethreesevenfive
Hyper treadmill pushing, panting
Swing over to exercycle! Matching cards
Simple Sit Sort Sweat
Legs harder. Tail thrash. Faster go. Win this time
Breathe heavy harsh harsh
Percussing ears
Cards paws blur
Numbers grow more anxious start over.

A sloth. Clumsy. Cloying. Pushing. Puzzle pieces
Sooooo slowly. I contemplate
Cardboard clues. Colours...spaces...shapes
Matching. No. Wait? Maybe.
Separated, scattered across the square table. So quiet
I stare. One time I think
I should look for edges
That's how you start.

****

This day HUBBY arrives appointed to meet
With me and the very doc HE protested
I see HIM in a room alone
I slither past and from the hallway
        Hiss "Are YOU going to tell the TRUTH?"
HE looks startled--I recoil, flee and return to strike
again
From the doorway spitting venom:
        "About SEX!--Tell THE secret?"

HE is alarmed—IT is never to be spoken
What if I finally told someone? What if I was believed?

Recomposed as the doctor attends
HE greets deferentially, deathly calm, concerned
        I rattling hard
        Trying to contain pull force my essence
        Into solid matter on a chair.

HE did not mention
"The (unfortunate) menopause". Instead
My PARTNER coos that I often threaten suicide
Laments that I never support HIS projects
Wistfully assures that my current state
Is perfectly normal for me.

        Exploding, flashing, screaming!
I choke out HE makes me... And I said IT
Demands
Brutal sex
Whores me
To serve as HIS safe hetero buffer
Between HIM and HIS own feared fraternal sexual
desire.

There was no air No need to breathe
        I SAID IT.
        The poison burst splattered disintegrated
        Boundless radiant light freed
        That only I discern.

Shrugging HE smiled slightly smug and settled back to
share
Impunity

An affable brotherly confession–
"Oh sure, we've always engaged in 'EDGY SEX'"
Minimised the abuse
Denied the violence
So clumsily stated
By a hag.

How could a kindred ego blame HIM?
The doctor paused, then nodded slightly off centre and
Professionally opined marriage tips
Numb, I agreed accommodated acquiesced
To all THEIR blind words together
            As I pooled dense and formless
            Mercury illuminating beneath my chair
            Amalgamating elemental energies
Then released paternalistically into my HUSBAND'S
care
Despite brave objections from 'The Nurses' Station'
They knew.

                    ****

At home collapsing in the shower
Screaming out loud now raging
At a puzzle on the floor then voiceless
Deeply satisfied dragging my nails
Over wicker furniture peering
Into rocks on the wall
Void green grey screen in my Mind's Eye. Blinking.
Jolt-clang.   Cascading tremors.   Detonated. Crack
Boom. Blank.

A lone quiet clear thought
            Pharmacist will know--

The new anti-depressant
Rather than 'the menopause'?
SHE discovered and saved HIS wife's life
Lucky not to have been seizing
Benzodiazepines Ceased.
Cold. Turkey.

Psychiatrist physician prescription 'problem' parsed
Eventually carefully apologised
Safely removed from unnecessary drugs
My mind returned.

The opportunity for a DEVOTED minister
To 'Gaslight' HIS WIFE conveniently
Arranged to disappear my her own hand
So HE could be free to (gloat and) float
Upon sympathy for HIS tragic WIDOWED loss
Passed.
So close.

HIS anger remained
HIS control chained to my dark shame and humiliation
HIS intrigue in secret games and tests of
Devotion and trust in HIM
Outed once, twice thrice,
Deeper violence and more nightmare clarity
        HIS filth regurgitated and purged but for scars.

The PREACHER'S demon
Secrets unleashed from HIS dungeon
Exposed to the light withered
        Lost all power over
        MY mind MY body MY spirit
        Never to be confined or confused by abuse nor

Driven to a chemical cliff again

Proudly, healthfully, and very energetically
MENOPAUSAL!

Unbearable

Shadows hidden locked
Raw Nerves
Under constant chatter   confusion   chaos
Over endless dread   angst   unease
Lies forgotten unknowing

Violated Soul, Mind, Body – iterative seasons eternal
echo
Cool, edgy sex his right?
His 'Cock Drunk' story time adopted by
Costumed hooded puppet slave bound in pornographic
love
Escape to peace
Unbidden instinct involuntary uncompelled
unconscious
Trauma unfurled shock stress
Blank slate now writing over-filled spilling trickles then
torrents
Unlocked nightmare threats loosed memories
Immersed in blaspheme
Suffocating in profanity
Obliterated by obscenity
Drowning in curses
Asphyxiated
Damned

No One Won

You felt you lost my undivided attention when our first
child was born
You felt you lost when my education challenged our
religious beliefs
You felt you lost when I chose faith and feminism over
patriarchal control
You felt you lost when my work gained respect in our
industry
You felt you lost when I balanced family, home, career,
farm and volunteerism
Did you truly win as you chased sex, money, and
accolades?
You felt you lost anytime my other interests began to
look successful
Did you truly win when you co-opted and took credit
for my efforts?
You felt you lost when I listened to anyone but you
You 'pious' Mormon felt you lost when I was able to
venture to speak up for myself

You truly lost when I finally released the sexually
deviant secrets that shamed me and emboldened your
impunity and control over me
You truly lost as I painfully learned and understood
why you punished and abused me all those years
You truly lost when I stopped covering for you and
others remembered, contemplated the missing pieces,
and watched you as you demonstrated your anger,
destruction, and deceit
NO ONE WON. You are brilliant, but our life together
was never a competition
You are left with all that ever mattered to you
And you truly lost everything that is important

Sorrow Song

Bottomless hole sole wailing grief
Bleak hope in hell's barren fear-laden silo
Lay down resistance; Release control illusion
Sigh-accept fevered anguish
Silence no Sorrow Song
Honour you who, as, where
Shattered nightmare present
Violated remains sifting ash
Now only allow enduring reality

Nature's reprieve; Transient wonderment hold
Chilly morning raindrops weaving lace in stillness

Taut reverberations pulsate, palpitate, cry
Resonate to waking essence
Cleanse Refresh Breathe

Slow, sacred smoke mingled voice raise despair to
ancestor skies
Sweat, weep tears, seep misery, discharge, entrust to
Mother Earth

Pregnant pledge in vibrant emerald scented shoots
Glimpse future
Focus prism briefly

Single wavelength sung full
Tenuous   Delicate   Fragile
Depths resurge, ebb flow, transform as first and
Each potential Phoenix particle promises

Ages crawl toward wingedness
Unfinished Spirit leads
Transcendent awareness
Share Sing Dream
Infinite whole soul healing belief

Autumn Run

Just now:
Running between the raindrops
      as Maples feathered me
       with gold, luminous yellows, scarlets.
Footfalls muted, splashing through a carpet of russet,
burgundy, browns.
Ahead a variety of orange, yellow, plum, ruby and
crimson
      against the stoic evergreens
      and the as yet cheerful and tenacious emerald
grass!
Quenching my soul!

A Word with Myself

I met her--My former life partner's replacement of me
Last night.   In a dream

She acquiesced when I requested a moment with her
In a place where she felt safe
Uninvited, barely noticed, he scrambled behind us

She and I sat gazing across from one another
Her beautiful turquoise eyes brightly attentive
He stood silently intruding over me
Pressing himself in at me from behind
Trying to signal, distract her

At first her mother and sister protectively flanked her
To bear with her
Her wary brother sat on the periphery
All three receding as they witness
Our encounter

She and I explored
Genuine, encouraging, delighted in each other
As his fear grew he leant in harder
I reached back and brushed him away
I spoke truth, and she nodded thoughtfully
Her spirit undistracted by his mischief darkening,
threatening
Unable to steal her
Forevermore

River rocks nestled beneath
Blazing sun shattered surface

Granddaughter guide igniting
MY SOUL REMEMBERING:

Gliding mingling star beams
Pure, luminous energy

Settling breath wrapped within earthbound home vessel
Caressed in gentle current sway

Water cradled amidst brilliant gems
Unique compositions

Pressed in time, compounded through ages
Polished for eternity

Heavens creation ebb and flow
Belongingness quenched

Communion of awe

Jessie Blair

Jessie Blair is of Mohawk and Irish/Scottish ancestry. She studies First Nations culture and history at the University of British Columbia. She enjoys learning from the Elders and attends as many cultural events as she can. Her short story *Back to the Land* is featured in the *Anthology for a Green Planet* (Filidh 2014) and her short story *Fundamental Challenges* is featured in *The Unvalentine Anthology* (Filidh 2015). *Blood is Not Enough* is her third successful submission. She lives with her husband in Vancouver, British Columbia.

Blood is not enough

Uncle Jack was unabashedly vocal about his views on women. His short white hair crowned his aging face and brought out his best features. He retired from electrical engineering just a few years ago. Whenever he voiced his misogynistic views, most women in the family just rolled their eyes at him, except for me. I am a middle-aged social worker, and I don't like Uncle Jack tormenting the women in the family. I, too, make my family roll their eyes whenever I hold my Uncle Jack accountable, because they perceive me as taking what he says too seriously--whatever that means.

Things really started becoming a mess between at a family gathering at my parents' house. My head turned towards the roar of laughter from a group of men that sounded like a tribe of monkeys following their leader. It was Uncle Jack telling one of his jokes.

Uncle Jack said, "I told my wife that every woman should get help in getting their driver's licenses by renewing their bus passes."

I overheard him. My chin went down; my eyebrows flattened; I frowned, and my lips pursed.

My sister Simone was standing next to me. She shifted her body to the left and crossed her arms. She looked at me with wide eyes and furrowed eyebrows.

She said, "Here he goes again. I hope he doesn't say anything humiliating about me."

I said, "I hope not."

Uncle Jack's lips tucked into each mouth corner to form a smirk. His eyes roamed around the room and fell upon Simone and me.

I said to Simone, "Brace yourself, the dark cloud is heading our way."

Simone gasped, she turned her back to Uncle Jack and crossed her arms in front of her body.

Uncle Jack: "Don't worry Simone, I'm sure the police will let you have your license back as soon as you can show them that you can drive within the yellow lines on the road."

His mocking laughter sounded like a crow derisively cawing.

Simone's head went down, and she closed her eyes as she struggled with herself to be patient.

I said, "That's awful! She's a good driver! She didn't get her license taken away. She was in an accident, and it was the other driver's fault!"

Uncle Jack put his hands on his hips and said, "Lighten up, Sonya! I was just joking."

"Your joke is not funny."

"You are sensitive today. Do you have your monthly visitor?"

"Just because your joke is not funny does not mean that I am on my period."

I shaped my thumb and index finger into an "L" on my forehead.

Uncle Jack looked at the men around him.

"Dumb broads have no sense of humour."

Some of the men pulled their heads into their shoulders and half smiled, other men's eyes grew large as they looked away.

"Asshole."

Uncle Jack's irises seemed to turn black, his chin went down, his eyebrows flattened and his mouth tightened so much that the skin puckered out. He put his hands on his hips.

My Dad intervened and said, "Stop this! Just walk away from each other. I will not have another evening ruined because of you two."

"Why am I silenced when I call him on stuff?"

"I am not taking sides. Sonya, just walk away."

I shook my head and stamped my feet as I walked away.

Later that evening as I was trying to meditate, my mind kept ruminating over the evening's argument like a broken record. My eyes filled with tears from the stress of it all. I could not face myself because I felt too guilty about my reaction to Uncle Jack's words.

Doing some restorative yoga poses first would be helpful, I thought. After yoga, I tried again to meditate. As I began the meditation, I closed my eyes, took a deep breath and exhaled. I repeated that process three times before realising that my mind was still focusing on Uncle Jack. Nobody ever silences him. I caught myself spiralling down into an emotional murk again, so I quickly brought my attention back to my breath. I began to chant Om Shanti to distract my mind.

Physically hurting Uncle Jack was not going to solve my problem, but I could not get it out of my head. Playing a meditation CD seemed to calm my mind. Each chime of the Tibetan singing bowls brought me into a deeper tranquil state. The guide's voice had a soothing tone, and she spoke of not judging your thoughts while you are meditating, but instead, accepting the thoughts and feelings and thanking yourself for being aware of your thought process. I hit rewind and listened to that part again several times as though repetition would engrave it on my soul. Empowerment came to me with the message that I could not control what anybody else says or does, and that includes Uncle Jack.

The next morning I met up with my sister Simone at a coffee shop. We were enjoying the moment until we saw Uncle Jack enter. I slid down into my seat as my shoulders slumped forward when he decided to join us. He sat straddled a chair.

Uncle Jack said, "Simone, you are such a nice young woman. You can take a joke with gentle good humour, unlike Sonya, who I am sure is still holding a grudge toward me."

Simone's jaw gaped open, and her eyes got wide. I began picking imaginary lint off of my top.

Simone said, "Uncle Jack, I do not feel comfortable."

"It was a compliment."

I said, "Yeah, it was a compliment to Simone but not to me."

"Why should I compliment you?"

"I did not say that you had to compliment me, but insulting me will not help our situation."

Uncle Jack said, "Your mother spoiled you. No wonder you do not get along with anybody."

I moved my hand in a swooping motion towards Uncle Jack as though trying to brush him away from me.

I said, "Uncle Jack, your thinking cap is so small that it is cutting off circulation to your brain."

Uncle Jack pointed his finger at me.

"Now you listen here, young lady. The world will not give special treatment to women like you just because you whine about inequality."

"When was the last time you actually had anything positive to say about women, including your wife?"

Uncle Jack stared coldly at me but said nothing.

"That's what I thought. No wonder your wife drinks."

Uncle Jack said, "How dare you! She does not drink that much."

"Yeah right, it is 11:00 a.m., have you checked her blood alcohol level yet?"

Uncle Jack pointed at me again.

"Stop right there, young missy. That was a low blow. At least I am married, whereas you will be single for a long time yet because nobody likes a screechy female."

"Nobody likes a dumb-ass male, either."

Simone started shaking when she noticed that people were starting to look at them. She spoke softly with her palms up towards both of us.

Simone said, "I think we all need to walk away from this conversation. We are attracting needless attention to ourselves."

Uncle Jack said, "I am just leaving."

Uncle Jack walked out of the coffee shop.

I said to Simone, "Silence is permission."

"Silence can be golden too."

I shook my head and then left.

That evening I was meditating at home. The cool air passed through my nostrils and filled my lungs, and I breathed out warm air. My body became increasingly limp as I sank deeper into relaxation. Memories of the arguments over the past two days clung to my mind like hungry leeches. My attempts at deep breathing were replaced by shallow breaths. My muscles became tense. I began to chew my fingernails. I hated that he could get under my skin. I hated him and everything that he stood for – the privilege of saying whatever he wanted without being challenged by hardly anybody, the proverbial unapologetic white man who believes that the world owes him: I was tired of it all. After several attempts at trying to meditate, I took myself out for a walk to calm down.

I walked into a late night café. As I settled into my seat, I noticed a sign on the wall with the *Serenity Prayer* on it. My eyes kept reading the words on the sign, "to accept the things that I cannot change". The waitress came by with my order.

The waitress said, "Let it go."

"I beg your pardon?"

The waitress said, "Your bagel."

"Oh, thank you. For some reason, I thought you told me to let it go."

"Let what go?"

My head tilted to the side, and my eyes became wide. The universe was sending me a clear message.

I said, "Nevermind."

The waitress' head went back; she raised an eyebrow and left the table.

The smell of butter melting on the bagel made my mouth water. I closed my eyes and smiled widely as I savoured that first bite. Nothing beats the taste of sweet butter melting on toasted bread. I took a deep breath after I swallowed. My uncle's words kept circling in my head like a hamster on a wheel. I admitted to myself that arguing with him was pointless because I cannot control what he thinks and says.

A week later my perspective had changed. I had not argued with Uncle Jack whenever the family gathered together. I noted that Uncle Jack was quieter these days, which was better than hearing his idiotic drivel. My winning streak was about to end family dinner that night.

Uncle Jack came and stood beside Simone and me.

Uncle Jack said, "The only nice woman is a quiet woman, right, Sonya?"

"The only nice misogynist is a lobotomized one."

The room rocked with laughter at my comeback. Uncle Jack put his one hand on his hip and pointed at me with the other hand.

"That is how you feminists prefer men, isn't it?"

Uncle Jack clenched his pointed hand into a fist.

"You need to be muzzled like the bitch that you really are."

I crossed my right arm in front of my body and stroked my throat with my left hand. My head was level as I locked eyes with Uncle Jack.

The house went quiet. I heard a dish smash on the floor.

My father said, "Could we not do this?"

"Dad, your brother just said that I am a bitch that needs to be muzzled. If you do not agree with what he said then tell him so."

My father went quiet.

"I do not like being caught in the middle."

I looked at the ground and rubbed my hands together. My face now flushed and the veins on my neck stood out.

"Very well, I will leave."

I grabbed my coat and left, much to my father's chagrin. My emotions were swinging as much as my arms as I walked home that night. I could feel the tension leaving my body and a wave of calmness replacing it. The emotional exhaustion of fighting for respect fell upon deaf ears. I heeded the wisdom of my sister's and father's words to walk away. I accepted myself without passing any further judgement for arguing with Uncle Jack. Being a blood relative was not enough of a reason for me to remain in a hostile environment.

Kenton Moore

Kenton Moore loves to tell stories. He loves it so much, in fact, that story-telling has become more than what he is known for. It is also who he is. Writing since the age of 16, Kenton has explored screenwriting for film and short film, and writing for animation and comic books. Most recently, he has taken a keen interest in books and short stories. He has a few journalism credits to his name, he's self-published children's novella, *Legend of the Sunlight Prince*, and actively operates a blog/magazine called *Great Northern Gothic*. He lives in Victoria, Canada, where he earns his daily bread as a Military Logistician and enjoys spending his free time with his two kids.

Kenton's story *The First* was previously published on his blog Great Northern Gothic.

Learn more about Kenton's work on Facebook @KentonMooreBooks, or #writethedarkness.

The First

It was the smell of the blood that got to me. Metallic yet somehow stale, almost like the horrible smell frying liver made back when Mom cooked it for me all the time. My left hand instinctively cupped under my nose, as my right lifted the yellow police line tape so I could duck under it. The front door of the house opened into an open-concept living room with a stairway to the left which led upstairs. Detective Rainier Tremblay held out a small jar of Vapo-Rub as I approached, retrieving his pen from his pocket after I accepted the cream. My eyes followed his briefing around the details of the room as I dabbed some Vapo-Rub on my finger and applied it to my upper lip. Sure, it made my eyes run, but it did wonders for the smell.

"Two victims. Adult female, age 37, stabbed numerous times," I followed Tremblay's pointing pen to my right where I could make out the horribly mangled remains of a blonde woman lying awkwardly between the couch and a glass coffee table. Medical examiners and CSI photographers were crawling all over the scene, cataloguing every shred of evidence they could find, while yet more personnel analysed the spray patterns of the blood all over the room; and I meant all over the room.

"What a mess…" I whispered, interrupting Tremblay's briefing. Tremblay simply looked at me and shrugged.

"One point five gallons in the human body…I'd bet she has little left in there."

One point five gallons. The room looked as though a third-year fine-arts student high as hell on whatever mind-bending drug is cool these days had turned the space into some kind of statement on the way our consumerism is destroying the planet. And that smell. Even through the Vapo-Rub, it was enough for me to have to consciously focus on not gagging. Red ran in streaking arcs across the floor, the walls, and even in spots across the ceiling. Yellow evidence photography tags were everywhere.

The medical examiner standing over the victim stood and shook his head. Even with all his protective equipment on, I recognized him right away. He looked over at me and Tremblay as he wiped sweat from his forehead with the back of his wrist. I liked him. He always managed to see things we missed. He would always joke about it being because he's Asian. Called it his "Asian racial bonus." Plus two to math and sciences. I had no idea what the hell he was talking about, but I liked him anyway.

"I count nineteen stab wounds to the torso and neck. Won't know for sure how much more there are everywhere else until we get her back to the morgue and clean all this blood off."

"Good work," I said. "We'll finish our sweep and then release the crime scene. Have the coroner get ready to move her."

I was just going through the motions. The scene was so grisly; I would have loved to authorise the coroners to move her right away. It almost felt like I would be doing the deceased a courtesy. No one deserves to have their life cut short. Especially like this. I looked at Tremblay, and his eyes met mine in a wordless request to continue with his briefing. I nodded and followed him across the living room floor past the art nouveau blood installation and into the kitchen area at the back. A large marble-topped island separated the living area from the tiled kitchen. There was blood here too, though in smaller spatters and mostly centred around a huge chef's knife that lay on the tiles near the fridge. The knife was of a single metal piece wherein the handle was moulded directly into the blade. At the base of the blade was a stamp that showed three prongs like those on a trident. It looked expensive, even though it was coated in blood and the tip had broken off.

"This is where we found the father. He was nearly catatonic, didn't respond to questions or stimuli in any way."

"Drugs?" I asked, taking my pen out of my pocket as I lowered to a squat. I moved the evidence photography tag that was casting a shadow on the broken tip of the knife.

"Don't know yet. They're running toxicology on his blood."

"Where is he now?"

"Back at the station. He didn't put up any fight at all. It was like he wasn't even here you know?"

I tapped the end of my pen lightly against the floor for a moment, pondering the angle of the knife and the bloody handprints on the counter to my right. I pictured for a moment how the man had leant against the counter before collapsing to his knees and dropping the knife to his side. I motioned to the broken tip with my pen before I stood.
"Do we know where that broken piece is?"

98

Tremblay nodded, and his jaw set for a moment. He sighed as if he didn't want to say what came next.

"M.E. thinks it's inside the second victim. Lodged in her sternum."

"Her? Another woman?"

"His daughter. Upstairs. Seven years old."

My heart leapt into my throat. I hated murder cases involving children more than anything else in the world, and Tremblay knew it. I suddenly realised why we had started downstairs, and why he had left out the second victim right from the outset.

"Nick...you don't have to..." Tremblay began, knowing the raging fire that was going on inside me. I pushed past him before he could bring up her name, or anything about her.

"Yes, I do. It's my job. Show me."

Rainier lowered his head and let me pass the kitchen island before following me back into the living room. Just before rounding the right-hand corner to begin climbing the stairs to the second floor, I hesitated. Tremblay moved past me and put his left foot up onto the first stair. He stopped and looked back at me, his eyes stern yet sympathetic.

"Are you sure, Nick? It's like *le diable's* playground up there..."

Without saying a word, I gestured with my pen for him to continue. Tremblay wasn't lying about his reference to the devil. I could feel my skin crawling more and more with each and every footfall up those stairs. The hair on the back of my neck stood up and sweat beaded on my forehead. I really had no idea what I would see, but at the moment I was focused on what I could feel. There was something ominous about the climb to the second floor, and even more so on the landing at the top. A presence was there, dark and terrifying, yet beyond my understanding. When we reached the end of the narrow hall, and Tremblay stood to the side of the door leading to the scene of the second victim's death, it took every ounce of courage I had to move past him and into the little girl's room.

Two things happened when that scene unfolded before me. One, I suddenly believed in the devil. And two, I added a half-digested pumpkin spice latte and an apple fritter to the fluid collection the medical examiners would be forced to perform. The darkness I felt was palpable. I could have cut it with a knife. I had been on the force for close to eighteen years, twice awarded for professional conduct, but the absolute depravity I saw before me was enough for me to chuck my cookies once more back out in the hallway while Tremblay desperately tried to return in time from the upstairs bathroom with some paper towel.

"*Tabarnak esti…*" Tremblay said, allowing some of his rarely used Quebecois to show. "I warned you."

I slowly came to my senses, and the world stopped spinning. Wiping the vomit from my mouth had also removed my thin layer of protection from the horrid smell of all the blood, so the first thing I did was retrieve the Vapo-Rub from my pocket and apply a liberal fresh coat. I sniffed deeply, allowing the vapour to expunge all the horror from my sinus, and then stood. I coughed a little, to ensure that the upset in my stomach was over. For now.

"Eighteen years, Rainier. Eighteen years and I never chucked my biscuits on a crime scene. Please tell me forensics has been up here already."

I could tell Tremblay wanted to laugh, and a huge part of me wished he would, but instead he simply ushered me back toward the stairs. I had no desire to go back in that room. What I saw would already be with me for the remainder of my days.

"They have. We were just waiting on your sweep to clear the scene."

When we reached the bottom of the stairs, my favourite Asian medical examiner was waiting for us, his goggles now hanging around his neck and his gloves removed. He looked at me inquisitively.

"Clear it. We're done here."

As he moved to give the coroners instructions, I reached out and grabbed him by the shoulder. He turned around and our eyes met. He had a faint smile, and I'm sure he knew already, but I told him anyway.

"I chucked my cookies up there... sorry."

He shrugged and patted me on the ribs under my outstretched arm resting on his shoulder.
"Hey... we can't all be perfect. Nice to know you're human."

I nodded and ducked under the tape that Tremblay was holding up for me. We walked silently down the concrete path that led up to the front door of the house. At the sidewalk, I stopped and turned to watch the beehive of activity as the crews prepared to clear the scene. The flashing lights from at least a half-dozen various emergency vehicles lit the house with an odd, almost festive glow of colours. From outside, the house looked so incredibly sterile: hanging pots, well-tended gardens on both sides of the porch stairs, a pink bike with training wheels and tassels dangling from the handles. I shivered, and for a moment, allowed myself to be mesmerized by the way those tassels reflected all the emergency lights. Then I turned to Tremblay.

"Okay... what the actual fuck goes through someone's mind to do...," I paused a moment, waving my hand in the air in circles as I tried to find a word. Finally, I simply motioned to the house, "...that!"

Tremblay shook his head. I could tell he had no more ideas than I did.

"It's crazy...," Tremblay began as he walked around to the driver's side of our unmarked squad car. "None of it makes any sense. Father loses it, completely butchers his wife and daughter, and then just... shuts down. Why didn't he touch the boy? That's what I don't get."

"The boy?" I asked as I opened the passenger door and slid into the seat. Tremblay slid behind the wheel and adjusted the seat. He was taller than me, and I had been driving last.

"Responders found a five-year-old boy just sitting on the stairs when they arrived. Untouched. Totally clean."

"Related to the perp?" I already suspected the answer, but Tremblay indulged me as he turned the car's ignition and dropped the transmission lever into drive.

"His son."

****

For one o'clock in the morning, the precinct was unusually abuzz when Tremblay and I arrived. Captain Turay came out of her office to greet us. She was wearing plain clothes, and her jet black curly hair was down in messy tangles. She was small in stature but made up for it with pure African-Canadian fury. Most of the men in the precinct called her Storm, after a comic book character, apparently. I didn't care where the name came from, because the moniker fit. She was a hurricane in her own right. Canting her hips to the side and resting her left hand on her waist, she gestured at me with her right hand, her coffee almost sloshing over the rim of her cup as she did.

"Nick… please tell me you didn't really heave your guts on a crime scene? And twice to boot? What's witchoo, boy?" She chided, the last part of her sentence accented with as much ghetto as she dared while on duty as Chief of Police.

"Fuuuuck…" I breathed, shaking my head in shame. "That made it here already, did it?"

"Mmm-hmmm. Kristoff called it in."

"Remind me to shave-bomb his locker..."

The Chief looked me up and down and spun away back toward her office. Tremblay and I followed.

"I didn't hear that," she said as she rounded her desk and sat down. Tremblay and I took seats opposite her. "He's off shift until tomorrow. Eighteen hundred hours. You didn't hear that!"

Tremblay and I shared a glance and shrugged.

"Hear what?" we said, almost in tandem.

Her point made, Captain Turay shook her finger in the air and took a sip of coffee.

"Helluva night out there. What we got?"

"Two dead. Adult female, thirty-seven years of age. Female child, approximately seven years of age. Both stabbed. A lot. Father is in custody, almost catatonic. A Five-year-old son in the hands of child services, found on the scene. We may need him for questioning."

I was grateful to Tremblay for taking the lead on this one. He was an excellent partner. I made a mental note to buy him a bottle of his favourite champagne to share with his wife. Captain Turay shot me a sympathetic glance.

"You need to speak to mental health about what happened tonight?"

The question caught me off guard. Made me realise I had spaced out for a few moments.

104

"What? No, I'm good, Captain. Locked and loaded."

Captain Turay nodded slowly, her words came slow and at low volume, but I could hear the tone of caring they carried.

"Locked and loaded…," she sat back in her chair and appraised the both of us, taking another sip of her coffee. "I want the child left in the hands of social services. Don't touch him unless you get nothing from the father, clear?"

We both nodded again.

"Alright. Let's put this to bed. Perp's in interrogation three if you boys are up to it?"

I looked at Tremblay, saw the resolve burning in his eyes. He never took his eyes off the Captain. Something about that look in his eyes told me he would forsake days of sleep if it meant closing this case. After what I had seen, I was right there with him. No words were spoken by either of us when I looked back at the Captain, but I could see the same look in her eyes as well.

"I'm going to need more coffee…," she sighed.

****

There was something completely unsettling about Thomas Barrow when Tremblay and I walked into interrogation room three. He sat completely motionless in the chair, arms draped at his sides with his cuffed wrists in his lap. His back was hunched over ever so slightly forward, and his head lowered to the point where his chin almost touched his chest. He very well could have appeared asleep were it not for his eyes. The haunting emptiness in their glazed stare was unnerving and gave the room a palpable chill.

"Thomas Barrow," Tremblay began, dropping the case file down on the desk with a thud. He was playing bad cop, and I was thankful for it. This whole case gave me the creeps. "Do you know where you are? You've been arrested for the murder of your wife and daughter."

Mention of the daughter brought a shudder to my already aching muscles. My stomach threatened to up-end, but I suppressed it as little more than a hiccup. Tremblay paused long enough to ensure I was okay as he paced the room behind Thomas.

"You were found at the scene, the murder weapon right beside you, covered in their blood. I have to say... it's not looking good for you Mister Barrow. If I were you, I would tell us everything we need to know. And fast."

"Mister Barrow," I began, allowing myself to fall into the routine Tremblay and I had perfected over our years together on the force. I sat down in the chair opposite Thomas. "Please. We need to understand what happened this evening. Can you tell us, Mister Barrow? Tell us what happened tonight at your home?"

Thomas Barrow did something then that made my blood run like ice-water through my veins. He twitched, a single spastic jerk, and dark black blood began oozing from his ears and down his jawline in thin rivulets. His jet black hair seemed almost alive.

"I killed the girl." he spoke quietly, his voice strained and broken, like someone who had been screaming for days at a rock and roll festival. "With the kitchen knife. Stab, stab, stab… then the woman. She ran. I chased. Downstairs I caught her. Stab, stab, stab, stab…"

"*Calisse tabarnak*!!" Tremblay exclaimed as he backed against the wall. I shoved my chair back from the table and leapt to my feet. Thomas Barrow continued to repeat the word stab over and over in that grating, broken voice of his. The blood from his ears was a river now, joined by tendrils from the tear-ducts of his eyes and a free flow from his nose. Suddenly, he simply stopped and opened his mouth. Grey-brown vomit rolled out unceremoniously and slid down the front of his shirt. There was nothing else.

I had no idea how much time had passed in silence as Tremblay and I stood in paralysed fear, but it was the sound of the door busting open that made us both jump and shout. Captain Turay was there, along with two beat officers I didn't recognise and my medical examiner friend.

"What in the actual fuck just happened," Captain Turay said, jabbing her finger at Thomas. "Check if that man is alive!"

The medical examiner stepped forward and pulled a surgical glove from his belt pouch first aid kit. He pulled the glove on with a snap and placed his index and middle fingers against Thomas' neck. The headshake he gave told us all we needed to know. Something had just killed Thomas in front of our eyes. Something none of us had ever seen before. Some new drug, perhaps. I looked over at

Tremblay, who was still backed against the wall and staring at Thomas.

"We didn't...," my words failed me, and my voice just seemed to trail off. Captain Turay spoke next, and suddenly I realised she had been watching from behind the two-way the whole time.

"I know, Nick. We were just on our way in to tell you the latest."

Tremblay seemed to snap out of his trance and looked from Captain Turay to the medical examiner and back.

"We?"

"Toxicology came back from the labs," the medical examiner stated. "And that's where things got really weird."

"Weirder than this?" I almost shouted, motioning to the corpse of Thomas Barrow.

"According to our toxicology reports... this man died nearly six hours ago."

"Impossible!" I barked, "That's before we even got the call!"

The medical examiner shrugged.

"Blood samples taken at the time of arrest to test for drugs showed his blood already congealed."

"Okay, enough," Captain Turay began. She turned to the examiner, "Get him out of here. I want a full autopsy ASAP." She turned to look at Tremblay, and then me. "This is some spooky shit."

I nodded my agreement and leaned back against the two-way glass. I felt that the Captain, at that moment, had a real penchant for understatement.

"What do we do?" asked Tremblay as he watched the examiner and the beat cop go to work bagging the body. Captain Turay ran her hands through her hair, then looked down at the medical examiner.

"Any chance whatever's going on is some infectious shit? Some... I dunno..."

"You mean like zombies?" the examiner asked.

"Yes. Like zombies." Turay was out of her element. I could see that. Hell... we all were.

"No," the examiner scoffed. "Tox was clean beyond the congealing."

Captain Turay thought for a long moment before turning to face me. She was close; I could smell her late night sweat mixed with coffee breath. Still better than that house.

"We need answers here. Fast."

She paused a moment, tapping her finger against her chin before shoving that same finger into my chest.

"Bring in the boy. No matter what it takes."

I nodded, and she turned and walked out of the room, following the body bag being carried by the M.E. and one of the beat cops. I turned to look at Tremblay, who was staring at the chair Thomas had sat in. Black blood and specks of the grey-brown vomit dotted the chair. We both gagged and bolted from the room.

****

By the time we were ready to bring in the boy, the entire goddamn province was all over the story. Word had spread like wildfire about a white-picket-fence man living the Canadian Dream who suddenly snapped and butchered his family, sparing a little boy, the case's sole lead. Despite the sudden prestige of the whole affair, we were given time to go home, rest, and shower. Shower, I did. For quite a long time, in fact, and accompanied by a straight bottle of whiskey. Rest? That part not so much. The story was all over the news, and when I finally arrived back at the precinct for the interrogation, I had to make my way through a whole throng of reporters. Thank God, I thought, that none of them knows about the puke.

Inside the Captain's office, Tremblay leant against the wall, arms crossed. He was unusually silent. Captain Turay paced back and forth. She was in her full dress uniform, probably because she expected to make a statement following the interrogations. Media frenzy and all that. She looked up with a sympathetic smile as I entered the room.

"The vultures outside didn't tear any meat from you, did they?"

110

I shook my head. I knew how to deal with the press.

Shortly after me, a tall blonde woman in a crisp business suit entered the room. Amy Ryanson, the district attorney. She was a livid bitch, almost impossible to please and way too happy to throw around threats, which only got worse.

"Has the boy arrived?" Amy barked, her sultry voice masking the venom she always spewed.

Captain Turay shook her head, but before she could speak, Amy was barking again.

"Who is leading the interrogation?"

My throat caught when Captain Turay said my name. Amy turned on me, and I instinctively averted my eyes. She was like Medusa somehow; her gaze made most men freeze. Not turn to stone, obviously, but freeze in other ways. She just had a way of depowering people. I figure that's how she became district attorney in the first place. I knew what was coming next, and it made my blood boil.

"I want someone else on this. Detective Perega is not fit to conduct this investigation, and I don't think I need to explain why."

I could no longer keep my eyes turned away. The surprise that flooded through me brought a powerful wave of confidence, along with something else. Rage.

"Oh," I retorted, my voice barely hiding the fury building inside me. "I very much think you do need to explain, Amy."

"Very well," she began, as she moved towards me. She was catlike, full of posturing and bravado. She swayed her hips as though swishing her tail, readying to pounce, but my anger wouldn't back down.

"You're too close to this. Too emotional. Do you really expect to successfully interrogate a child when only a year ago, you buried your own?"

There it was. I knew it. This bitch had been on my tail ever since our daughter's accident, trying in some way to prove that her "useless detective ex-husband" was responsible for her death. She always went back to this. Always. I had simply had enough.

"Enough with this bullshit!" Captain Turay shouted.

Amy stopped inches from my face, and I could feel the hatred burning behind her sky-blue irises. She blamed me. She always would. I saw her lip quiver for just a moment; saw a hint of moisture rim her eyes. I gritted my teeth so hard that I heard them squeak, and she heard it too.

"You two need to stow your shit, and stow it NOW!" Captain Turay hollered. "I got half the media in central Canada outside my precinct, and I need my lead detective and our D.A. to do their bloody jobs!"

I didn't need to say a word. My eyes said it all, and after a long moment of testing each other's resolve, Amy backed down.

"Fine," Amy said as she barged out of the office. "Don't blame me if he fucks up again. I warned you."

Tremblay breathed a massive sigh of relief as I lowered my head and idly stroked my ring finger. It was Captain Turay who broke the ice.

"Suck it up, Nick," she said, her tone softer and sympathetic. "We know the truth, and you have a job to do."

As the Captain made her way around the desk and strode to the door, Tremblay and I fell in behind her.

"Don't know what the fuck you ever saw in that one, Nick…" Turay whispered under her breath.

I couldn't help but let a little smile creep into the corner of my mouth as we all headed for the interrogation rooms.

****

Nathan Barrow was just like any other five-year-old boy I'd ever met. He was pure innocence, sitting on the chair in the interrogation room playing with a toy train and police cruiser. He was smiling, his short brown curly hair a pleasant medium of his Father's black and his Mother's blonde. His police cruiser chased the train calling for the robbers to stop because they had stolen a train. A representative from social services and a trauma counsellor stood at the back of the room near the door, whispering and watching like hawks. I sat across from Nathan, the same way I had sat across from his father. The thought of Thomas made me shiver. Behind the glass, I knew that Amy, Tremblay, the Captain, and probably a host of others were watching intently, so I wasted as little time as I could.

"Hello, Nathan. My name is Nick."

"Hello!" Nathan cooed as the police cruiser finally managed to crash into the train, sending it flipping across the table, to the astonishment of the robbers.

"Nathan, I need to ask you some questions. Do you think that would be okay?"

"Sure."

"Nathan…," I nervously glanced at the trauma counsellor and the social services rep. The trauma counsellor nodded that it was okay for me to proceed. "Nathan, something very bad happened yesterday, and I know you may be too scared to talk about it, but we need to understand what happened. Can you tell me what happened when your mom and sister were hurt?"

I felt completely uneasy, and a wave of cold fear washed over me. How could I expect a five-year-old child to understand what I was asking of him? How would he have interpreted those horrific events in his growing mind? I glanced again at the trauma counsellor and saw no disagreement.

"Daddy went through the breaking, and he killed Mommy and 'lizabeth."

My heart felt as though it had stopped in my chest. My skin was now akin to the surface of the moon, with goosebumps distorting my flesh. The temperature in the room felt suddenly arctic, and when I turned my head toward the mirror behind me and then to the counsellors, I could clearly see I was not alone. Nathan had stopped playing and sat bolt upright, completely engaged and nonchalantly talking about his family's murder as though it were a game he was playing. Maybe it was.

"The breaking?" I squeaked, surprised at the frailty of my own voice.

"Yes. Chadwick showed me how to do it. I can't do it yet... because I'm still alive... so Chadwick did it to Daddy to show me how it's done."

I swallowed hard, but my mouth and throat felt like ash. Five-year-old children have incredible imaginations; I knew that much. Especially after seeing the way he played out the scene with the train robbers and the police cruiser, but something about the sincere innocence he was portraying here was beyond terrifying.

"Can you tell me where we can find Chadwick?"

"Chadwick lives on the other side of the veil. He's kinda like a ghost? Only he's real because he talks to me."

At the mention of ghosts, I relaxed a little bit, even if this whole situation was something from the Twilight Zone.

"Could I talk to Chadwick, Nathan?"

Nathan shook his little head, thought for a moment, and then shrugged. This naturally child-like body language made the interrogation seem even more bizarre.

"No… maybe… I dunno. It's hard for him to talk to me. He can only do it when he holds me in that spot between asleep and awake. Chadwick says that place is like a skin between us and the veil. Some people get trapped there when they die, and Chadwick knows how to use them. It's why we sometimes talk to people who have died in our dreams. Like Sandra."

This time I actually felt a palpable pain squeeze the inside of my chest. My heartbeat hammered in my ears, and my vision blurred. I knew it was because my eyes had become wet with tears.

"You miss her, don't you, Nick? Sandra Perega. Your daughter?"

At that moment, time slowed to a stop. I was vaguely aware of a muffled thump and some distant yelling from behind the mirror. It was all I could do to stare at the little boy sitting across from me. The little boy who, when I came in had seemed such an innocent child playing with his toys. The little boy who had spoken of ghosts. The little boy who had spoken of my dead daughter.

The door blew open, but I didn't take my eyes off the boy. Amy shot into the room like a ballistic missile headed straight for the boy, and still I didn't flinch. The counsellors tried to intercept her, but they collided with Captain Turay

116

and Tremblay as they thundered into the room behind Amy. The boy and I kept our eyes locked together, my breath coming in ragged pulls while he calmly looked back at me. Those innocent eyes. I heard his voice, though it was clear his lips weren't moving.

Do you want to see the breaking, Nick? Chadwick can show it to you.

Amy was viciously shaking Nathan and screaming, but it sounded like an echo in a public pool when you are underwater. Even as the boy was thrashed around by Amy, and the others tried desperately to pull her off of him, his eyes never left mine.

The breaking won't hurt, Nick. You could see Sandra again. Would you like that, Nick?

A single, ice-cold tear rolled down my cheek, and at that moment I heard a new voice inside my head, as the world exploded around me.

"Close your eyes, Dad."

I did.

In the darkness, I saw a faint form take shape ever so slowly, as if made of light and smoke. Like in a dream, I couldn't make out details, but I knew in my heart it was her. I felt peace and warmth wash over me like a hot shower after a cold winter run.

"Sandra…"

"Hi, Dad. Don't worry about me, okay? I'm fine. You need to stay away from that house. Stay away from that boy. Avoid the breaking, Dad… at all costs. Promise me."

"I promise. But… how is this even real?"

"I can't explain, Dad. It just is."

"You're a ghost…"

"Yes."

"Does it hurt?"

Sandra laughed, a sweet sound filling my head like gentle chimes in a summer breeze.

"No. It doesn't hurt Dad. But I have to go now. You have to go."

"Why?"

"I don't have answers for you, Dad."

"What is the breaking, Sandra?"

"Nothing good, Dad. Promise me you'll stay away."

"How can I stay away? So much has happened…"

"You'll know when you open your eyes."

"What does that mean?"

"Dad, I have to go. Promise me."

"Okay, Sandra... I promise I'll stay away.

"Thank you..."

"Sandra?"

"Yes?"

"I..."'

"I know, Dad. It's not your fault. I love you."

Then she was gone, and I was alone in the darkness behind my eyes. The comfort of her presence remained, however, and when I opened my eyes, I was standing in front of Thomas Barrow's house, back at that moment before Tremblay and I had left the crime scene. I blinked my eyes rapidly, trying to comprehend what had just happened. Festive emergency lights once more blinking against the walls, the strange, eerie serenity of it all flooded in, and I drew a deep breath.

Part of me half expected to wake up suddenly inside the interrogation room again; where all hell had broken loose because of one strange boy and his ghost story. Instead, the air in my lungs carried the burning scent of Vapo-Rub and the faint odour of blood and vomit.

I was back before it all had happened. This was real. I caught a shimmer on the grass near the path; let myself get lost in the reflections of those tassels on the pink bike again. Somehow, whatever Sandra had done had lifted a dreadful weight inside me. Maybe it was her assurance that her accident wasn't my fault. Maybe it was being put back before it all happened. Maybe it was everything all at once. Somehow, deep down inside me, I felt a spark. I felt a rebirth, if such a thing is possible.

"It's crazy…," Tremblay began as he walked around to the driver's side of our unmarked squad car. "None of it makes any sense. Father loses it, completely butchers his wife and daughter, and then just… shuts down. Why didn't he touch the boy? That's what I don't get."

I let the events that had transpired wash over me in rapid succession. Thomas' interrogation, the media frenzy, the fight with Amy, Nathan, Sandra. It couldn't have been a dream, could it? I knew it wasn't, but I had no explanations at all for how I knew. Something had happened, whether it was Nathan, Chadwick, or Sandra, and I was back here again. At the beginning. Maybe I'll never know how or why, but I do know that somehow… someway… this was real. I sighed, taking one long look at the house.

"Hey," Tremblay said from the other side of the car. "You okay, Nick?"

I turned and faced him; offered the best smile I could muster and hoped he didn't see through it.

"Yeah. I'm good. What did you say?"

"I said I don't get this. Why'd the father lose it? And why spare the boy?"

"I don't know," I said, as I opened the passenger door and slid into the seat. "I just know I don't want to touch this case with a ten-foot pole. We got the guy at the scene red-handed, no pun intended. Best to leave well enough alone. Let's call it in. File reports in the morning."

"You sure Turay will like that? The perp's in the station waiting on interrogation…"

"I'll explain it. This one's on me. I have a feeling he won't mind waiting for someone else."

Tremblay shrugged, started the car, and dropped the shift stick into drive.

"Crazy… a man going nuts like that."

"Yeah," I said. "Crazy how some people just… break."

Monique Jacob

Monique Jacob is currently writing the final instalment of her Cricket Lake trilogy, *Voodoo Café*, and has recently published *Bright Light*, a science fiction novel for teens.

Leaving the Cave is the story of a man who wakes up alone, with no memory of who he is or how he got there. In order to get home, Daren has to choose between the pull of the familiar and the siren call of the unknown.

Coming of Age is the opening scene of her upcoming novel *Immortal Dilemma*, where Joel discovers that breaking the rules can mean much more than just getting in trouble with your mom.

Her short stories, *Frankencycle* and *The Peanut Pit* are featured in the *Anthology for a Green Planet* (Filidh 2014). Her short stories, *First Responder* and *Mrs. Kwan,* are featured in *The Unvalentine Anthology* (Filidh 2015).

Go to https://MoniqueJacob.com for free story downloads and to her Facebook page for news and updates.

Leaving the Cave

one

When Daren came to, he was lying on hard ground. A thin layer of sand rasped beneath him as he instinctively eased away from the rocks poking his back. He was groggy, and a deep wave of tiredness threatened to drag him back to sleep, but the sharp rocks won, and he forced his eyes open.

His surroundings were in shadow except for a faint glow in the distance. Daren couldn't tell if he was really awake yet or if he'd fallen into another dream, the kind that shifts every time you think you've managed to claw your way back to the surface. He moved his arms out to the side, and the fingers of his left hand scrabbled along a rough stone wall.

Daren struggled to his feet, stiff and bruised, hugging the wall for support. The stone was damp at shoulder height and curved to a roof glistening with moisture a few inches above his head. He hunched reflexively and followed the wall to the spot of light.

The floor angled steeply upward, and Daren used an arm to shield his eyes as he emerged into the glare of a noonday sun. He crouched near the entrance, disoriented by the sudden change from cool damp to blistering heat.

Barren landscape, as far as he could see. Not a single tree or bush, not the slightest trace of greenery. Nothing but brown dunes undulating in orderly rows like static ocean waves.

Daren scooped a handful of hot sand and let it sift through his fingers. It felt real enough. "Where the hell am I?" The words were barely whispered, but they settled the issue of whether he was asleep or awake. Daren was always silent in his dreams.

Panic drove him to his feet and away from the cave, running up and down endless sand dunes until he was gasping for breath. He finally staggered to a stop at the top of a mound and turned in circles, scanning every direction for some familiar landmark.

Heat rose from the baking sand, hazing the horizon. The only imperfection in the sculpted landscape was the crooked line of footprints linking him back to the cave.

Directly across from the cave, at least three times further than the distance he'd already run, a vague form shimmered deep within the heat waves, wobbling and changing shape with every blink. Mirage or oasis?

Daren ran a dry tongue over chapped lips and turned to his cave, whose dark doorway beckoned silently with the promise of relief from the relentless sun. Maybe there were answers inside, and he should have explored its depths instead of running out into a baking desert like an idiot. He glanced once more at the illusion swaying in the distance and retraced his footsteps to the cavern.

He shivered as the darkness enveloped him. The cave entrance was small compared to the gigantic desert, and he ran a hand along the wall to keep his bearings as he worked his way toward where he'd first awoken. The stone under his fingers became cooler as he moved away from the entrance, and he slid down the wall to sit with his eyes closed, willing himself to recall what had brought him here.

Had someone knocked him out and abandoned him, in the middle of nowhere? Daren rubbed his temples wearily. His mind felt numb, and he couldn't think straight. He hoped someone was looking for him but couldn't imagine who that might be.

The only sound came from the farthest depths of the cavern, where moisture dripped on stone. The monotony was soothing, and Daren let it lull him to sleep.

two

"I saw his eyes open for just a second!" Lisa hugged herself to stop shivering and backed out of the way so the doctor could examine Daren.

"It's an involuntary response. His brain is working to repair the damage it has sustained. You may see a few more twitches." He adjusted Daren's bandages. "There's nothing more to do now, except wait." The doctor left to continue his rounds. The door swung shut behind him.

Lisa stroked Daren's hand and leant over to kiss the tip of his nose, the only part of his face that wasn't covered in thick bandages.

three

A loud thumping vibrated through the stone floor. Daren stood and stretched his cramped muscles, fighting to hold onto the dream he'd been shaken from. He'd heard a woman's soothing voice speaking familiar words, but the fragile scraps faded before he could make sense of them.

He pressed his palms to his ears to keep out the noise– straining to retrieve more than the vague feeling of pain and loss he'd woken with–but the persistent beat eventually drove him outside, where his nerves thrummed from the combination of deep rhythmic pulse and searing light.

Daren spied movement several dozen metres to his left. A wavering line–a parade of sorts–was headed in the direction he'd previously taken. A drummer set a steady pace at the head of the group, blue and gold banners streaming out behind. The striding drummer's features twisted and writhed grotesquely, as if a fearsome creature had affixed itself to his face. It made him dizzy just to look at it, but the steady drumbeat compelled Daren to follow.

A dozen people trailed the drummer, some throwing nervous glances over their shoulders as they struggled to keep up. They weren't dressed for a hike in the desert. Men sweated in business suits, and women limped in their bare feet, having abandoned their shoes along the way. A few at the front of the line were in high spirits and clapped in time with the beating drum, occasionally breaking stride to run back and encourage someone who had fallen behind.

They were the only people Daren had seen in this lifeless place, and they were quickly moving away from him. He gave chase but soon faltered and stopped, glancing back at the cavern uneasily. He'd ventured much farther away from it than the last time.

But the group was just ahead. Daren could hear them whispering and panting in the heat. Real people—not a dream—and they were headed for his distant mirage, which steadied and solidified as they approached. He gaped at the apparition and nearly stumbled over his own feet.

A stone fortress the height of ten men jutted up out of the sand as if it had grown there. The crenellated walls were topped with soaring towers, and its arched stone doorway was intricately carved with sharp-fanged beasts waging battle against winged beings with swords. The giant door swung open on silent hinges.

Daren finally caught up and jostled several members of the caravan before he managed to snag someone's attention.

"Please help me. I'm stranded here, and I don't know what's going on." He grabbed a woman's arm and forced her to stop. She gave him a radiant smile which faltered when he wouldn't let go, and Daren saw raw panic behind her joyful facade.

"I have to keep up with the others," she said, pulling away. "We finally found the city gates!" When she realised that he wasn't trying to stop her, she smiled again and took his hand. "My name is Shelley. Come with us."

"Do you know what's happened? I mean, I have no idea how I got here."

"Not really. Maybe. I'm just glad I'm out of that dark hole."

"Was it like a cave? I was in one too. What the hell is going on?"

"Come on, or we'll get left behind." Shelley tugged on his hand, urging him to keep up.

"I don't know if I can go with you. I'm not supposed to be here, but don't know how to get back, wherever that is." Daren had lost sight of the cavern. What if someone came looking for him, and he wasn't there? He'd miss his own rescue.

Shelley quickened her pace. "There's nothing left to go back to," she said bitterly. "The caves aren't meant to last."

The fortress walls soared high above the group as the gates lumbered open. A cool mist spilt out and curled around the foremost members of the group. Daren glimpsed beautiful buildings glittering through the haze, and in the distance, snow-capped mountains towered over everything. There were cries of wonder and laughter from the others. Shelly pushed forward, dragging Daren along with her.

But at the very entrance to the city, the moment the mist caressed his face, Daren panicked. He was certain that going through the gates would mean never returning to the cave, and never knowing how he might have got here. He pulled away from Shelley and stumbled back to the desert sand.

"Please come with us. This may be the only chance you get." Shelley reached out a hand but made no move to stop him.

Daren didn't care. He turned and ran, staggering and ploughing through powdery dunes in his haste to return to the safety of his cave. He didn't slow down until it wavered into sight. Only then did he pause to catch his breath and continue at a slower pace.

four

"How can you be so sure he's in a better place?" Lisa leant toward the chaplain, searching his eyes for answers.

"Daren didn't believe in any sort of afterlife. He thought that when you died, you just stopped being. Death terrified him."

"Just because he didn't believe in a higher power doesn't mean it doesn't exist." The chaplain set Daren's photo on the table next to the open coffin. "Daren led a good life. Have faith, Lisa. Paradise is open to everyone, even if one needs to touch it before accepting its reality."

Lisa wanted to believe that Daren continued to exist somewhere other than in her memories.

But paradise? No way. Daren would think he was hallucinating.

five

Daren's step faltered and he fell to his knees, breathing heavily. It couldn't be! He'd followed his fading trail of footprints back to his cavern, but its cool dark interior no longer beckoned him with a possible link to a home, a life.

The dune had collapsed, and the cave entrance was quickly filling with sand. He stumbled forward and frantically scooped double handfuls of hot sand, trying to shovel his way back in. He jammed his head into the dune, hoping to worm his way through the avalanche, but he soon had to pull out, coughing and spitting the scorching grains from his tongue. His face and hands were burned and blistered, and he fell to his knees, screaming curses at the sky.

Shelley was right. The cave had been only a temporary refuge. He felt hollowed out, and he wondered if this cavernous emptiness had only ever existed inside of him.

When his tears were spent, and his voice reduced to a hoarse whisper, he stood wearily and trudged back to the city that had offered refuge.

He should have had a raging thirst by now, but though his skin was burnt and his mouth as dry as the gritty sand that surrounded him, he felt no need beyond that of putting one foot in front of the other.

There was no way for Daren to tell time, as the sun was always directly overhead. The air shimmered wherever he looked, wavy lines coming off the sand and distorting the horizon. He kept his eyes on the ground as he retraced the path the group had churned into the sand. Eventually, the multiple footprints faded and smoothed into the rolling, endless dunes.

He tripped over an irregular hump sticking out of the sand and looked up to find that he was surrounded by debris. He'd been watching for the city in the distance and hadn't noticed that he'd arrived, that he was standing on it. The mighty fortress was in ruins.

Daren moaned and fell to his knees among the rubble. He picked up a piece of broken stone–decayed with age– and traced the faint outline of furled wings with a finger. He held it close to his chest, and the remains of the massive archway crumbled in his grasp. In the time it had taken him to travel to his cavern and back, the city had fallen. It hadn't seemed like a long time; Daren didn't feel like he'd changed at all since he'd last stood in this spot. He had missed his opportunity to enter the city.

Even worse, he had rejected it.

Daren was contemplating digging a hole and burying himself among the city's ruins when he spotted a flash of colour poking out of the ground next to his foot, like a fragile desert flower. He pulled at it, and familiar blue and gold banners streamed out of the sand, exposing a leather mask and drum lying underneath.

Daren tied the colourful banners to his belt and reached for the drum. Its rough edges shifted and smoothed where he stroked it, and as he nestled the drum under his arm, it moulded itself to his body's contours. He was oddly comforted by its bulk and lightly tapped the worn skin with a finger.

The resulting sound was impossibly loud in the still, hot air. Daren recognised the power of the tone that reverberated through his body as he struck the drum again. This was the irresistible beat that had drawn him away from his cave and led him to the city gates the first time.

A writhing form nudged his foot. Daren fumbled the drum and caught it before it hit the ground. It thrummed as

132

he clasped it to his chest and the mask responded by twitching in his direction. He had hoped to avoid the fearsome-looking mask, but it followed him as he backed away. It slid like oil across the surface of the sand and rested near his foot when he stopped.

He wasn't about to give up the drum—sensing that they wouldn't be separated, he gingerly picked up the mask. It was cool where he'd expected heat, and its edges fluttered, stroking his fingers. He closed his eyes and reluctantly put on the mask. It pulsated gently as it settled to the contours of his face. He kept still, afraid he'd be suffocated, but he could see and breathe clearly enough, and it soothed his burned skin. He rapped the drum again.

The mask moved, most of it oozing to the left side of his face. He felt roiling vertigo, as if he'd looked down from a great height. He turned to the left, and the mask slid back to cover his face evenly. His discomfort was immediately replaced by happiness so profound that tears sprang to his eyes.

Daren tested the mask once more by simply turning his head to one side, but elation and hope easily outweighed the lurching sickness he felt when he resisted, so he faced the direction it told him to and began a tentative rhythm. His head swayed forward, and he nearly tripped as his feet hurried to keep up. A few steps later he silenced the drum, and the mask eased its drag on him, resting lightly on his face, waiting patiently.

The mask and drum obviously wanted him to follow their lead, which made about as much sense as anything else he'd encountered in this place. They had brought

Shelley and the others to a glorious city and clearly wanted to lead him somewhere. There had to be other cities in this desert. He would find one.

There also had to be other caves, with people like him, lost and afraid. He'd find them, too. Daren wondered how many times the mask and drum had rescued people who were terrified to leave their caves. His fingers patted the drum's smooth top again, and he cried out joyfully when the mask gently tugged on his skin, showing him the way to go.

Resolutely turning his back on the crumbled city, the collapsed cave, and his lost memories, Daren set off in search of heaven.

Coming of Age

The attic was off-limits. But mama was sleeping, and the third floor beckoned. Joel crept up the stairs, and a nervous giggle escaping him every time a board creaked. The early afternoon sun beamed through the stained glass windows, creating a colourful mosaic on the wall. Most days, the sight mesmerised him, and he stroked the pretty colours until the sun moved, and the patterns disappeared. Today his gaze was riveted on the door at the top of the stairs.

Someone behind the door had whispered his name.

The latch was flimsy. No one had expected Joel to defy the rules and try to open the attic door. He twisted the doorknob with his left hand and twitched in fright as it opened, his crippled right hand jerking and rapping the wall sharply. A thin stream of urine ran down his leg, and he squeezed his eyes shut until he had control again of his bladder and his traitorous right hand.

"Big boy, big boy, big boy," he whispered as he snuck into the forbidden room, sneaking guilty glances behind him. He was terribly afraid, his mind conjuring visions of big, hairy spiders and boy-eating rats. But the pull was too strong to resist. Someone had whispered his name.

Muted sunshine struggled through the dirty windowpanes, lighting dust motes that floated in the stale air. Joel's distinctive footprints—with the toes of his right foot dragging through the dust - trailed behind him as he slowly moved deeper into the room. He flinched at every shrouded chair, his teeth chattering with fright when the old dust covers fluttered to life in the breeze of his passing. But not even the gloomy shapes looming throughout the long room were enough to dissuade him from answering the call of the voice that knew his name.

Rivulets of sweat ran down his chest and back under the striped wool sweater he insisted on wearing nearly every morning, regardless of the season.

But none of this—not the heat-choked air, not the throat-closing fear--stopped him from keeping a sharp lookout for spiders and rats. His mama would be very angry if he were to be eaten by a rat.

At the far end of the long attic room, behind a leaning wardrobe where the light barely penetrated, a large rug was tacked to the wall. Joel squeezed himself behind the wardrobe and brushed his fingers across the coarse wool. He forgot his fears for a moment, as he puzzled out how the floor had gotten onto the wall. How was he supposed to walk on it up there?

The voice whispered his name again, and his eyes widened as he realised it came from behind the rug. He grabbed the bottom corner with his good hand and heaved. The rug tore away from the nails, its weight knocking Joel backwards. He fell against the wardrobe, which teetered for an endless moment and then crashed heavily to the floor. A swarm of tiny mice vacated, running in every direction through the cloud of dust he'd churned up. He stumbled away from them in fright, in case they decided to eat him, and then tried to pick up the wardrobe one-handed, coughing hoarsely from the dust. But it wouldn't budge, so he turned back to the wall, squinting through the murk at what had been hidden behind the rug. He crept forward and ran his fingers along the edge of the heavily carved wood that framed a life-sized painting.

Then the painting called his name again, and he forgot all his fears about the attic: forgot the rats, the spiders, even forgot the trouble he'd be in for coming up here in the first place. As the dust cleared from the air, he was stunned to see his mother looking out of the painting. She was young and pretty and held a baby in her arms. But it was the man who stood next to her that drew his gaze. He stared at the man. This man had called his name. He knew this. It was his Papa. He knew this too. Joel laughed and slapped his thigh in excitement.

As he reached out tentative fingers toward the man's face, he didn't hear the attic door slam against the wall.

"Joel, no! Joel Brocard, you get away from there right now!" Lucinda thundered across the attic floor, horrified and furious. She grabbed at Joel's sleeve just as his fingers touched the canvas. Too late, she saw Simon's painted image waver, and her son's body sway closer.

"Please Joel, let's go. Time to leave," she begged, as she wrapped her arms around his chest and tried to pull him back. Simon's last will had stated that Joel was to receive the painting at the age of nineteen, but Lucinda was convinced that the boy was mentally unfit, and not able to appreciate it.

Joel was a week past his nineteenth birthday. How had he managed to find it so easily after ignoring the attic for so many years?

"Da! Da!" Joel cried, his voice high with wonder. His body was trembling and beginning to twitch all over, as it had when he was a small boy and prone to seizures.

"That's right, Joel, that's your Daddy. Let's go downstairs, and we'll look at it again later." He'd never seen a photo of his father since Simon had never allowed her to take one of him. How had Joel guessed that this was his father, a man he could not remember?

A ripple ran through the painting, continuing through his fingers into his body. He twitched and stiffened, then broke the contact as he fell heavily to the floor, taking Lucinda with him. The paint flowed across the canvas, swelling and surging in time with Joel's convulsions. His heels drummed on the pine floor, and his angelic features twisted with shock and pain. Lucinda pinned his arms to his sides and whispered reassurances, the only thing she knew to do for her feeble son.

She looked up at the painting, silently cursing Simon for dying and abandoning them when Joel was an infant. But the image had changed, and Simon's face was unrecognisable. The swirling paint had begun to run down the canvas and onto the floor. A colourful puddle seeped under Joel's body, oozing through his clothing and onto his skin. She could no longer clearly see Simon in the painting, though her younger self and baby Joel hadn't changed. A knot of fear tightened in her gut, and she wanted to run from the room. Run and never come back. Run and forget she'd seen the smile on Simon's face before it melted. A smile that hadn't originally been painted there.

Joel's spasms were slowing, and his breathing was quieter, evener. Lucinda brushed his curls away from his forehead and kissed his damp skin. He hadn't had a seizure in years; she would call the doctor later. Maybe his medication needed adjusting. Lucinda's mother suffered from seizures, and her brother had nearly died from one at a young age. Hughie had been sweet and slow, much like her son.

Joel stirred in her arms, moaning and grimacing. She helped him sit up and take off his sweater. It was soggy from paint, sweat, and urine.

"My poor baby," she crooned, as she pulled the rug closer and used a corner to clean his fingers. They were smeared with paint from when he'd touched the canvas. She ignored the small voice at the back of her mind that insisted that twenty-year-old paint shouldn't run as if it were fresh but made sure none of it touched her skin. "Let's go downstairs and have some hot chocolate. I'll bet we can even find a couple of marshmallows to put in it."

Joel smiled vacantly as he looked around him, dazed and surprised. Lucinda took his chin and turned his face toward hers. His lower lip hung slackly, and a pool of saliva threatened to spill over.

"Earth to Joel. Is anyone there?" The expression that never failed to make him laugh had no effect this time. He stared blankly at the ruined painting, his head tilted to the side.

He had his father's blue eyes, though Joel's were not as clear as Simon's, their sheen muddled by a lifetime of anticonvulsive drugs. Lucinda understood the need for the drugs but resented the toll they had taken on her son's personality.

She smiled in reassurance as he finally focused on her face. His expression changed rapidly from confusion, to surprise, then to awe as his eyes locked onto hers. She flinched, pulling back at the intensity that burned in his gaze. His eyes darted over her features, and a smile spread slowly across his face. Her stomach tightened another notch, and a cold finger of ice skittered down her spine. He raised his left hand and touched her cheek.

"Luce."

The word was garbled, like most of his speech, but even with the swallowed "L", and lisp at the end--sounding more like the word 'youth'--she recognised the name that only Simon had ever called her.

"No, Joel, I'm Mama. Remember? Mama," she said, inching away fearfully. What was wrong with her boy? Her pulse drummed loudly enough to hear as she scrambled to her feet, steering clear of the colourful paint swirls on the wooden floor. She had to call Wayne; he would know what to do, though he would be furious with her for allowing Joel to come up into the attic. He'd be certain to blame her, though she hadn't been up here herself since Simon died, hadn't ever given Joel any reason to come up the back stairs. Indeed, she'd made certain that Joel would fear the attic, having told him countless times that the third floor was filled with creepy, sticky spiders and giant rats that loved the taste of boy.

"Luce, my Luce," Joel said, slurring the words, and began to laugh in delight as he reached for her again.

Lucinda screamed and fled the attic.

Ron Kearse

Ron has led a nomadic life, having lived in most provinces in Canada. His resumé is varied and colourful--he's worked at everything from a tree farm in northern Ontario to assisting with special projects for a major resource company in Alberta and working with Aboriginal offenders in British Columbia's federal penal system.

Author, columnist, blogger, photographer and broadcaster, Ron has published two novels, *Road Without End* and *Just Outside of Hope*, along with a book of photographs called *Lost History*. His short story, *The Snow Falls on Montreal*, was published in The Unvalentine Anthology (Filidh 2015).

Ron is taking a hiatus from writing his third novel to travel the world writing, filming and taking photos with the memory of his partner, Steven Foster, by his side.

Somewhere There's A Field

July 31, 2015. I'll never forget that morning as long as I live. A phone call came from the Palliative Care Unit at Saint Paul's Hospital at 7:30, telling me I'd better get down there ASAP because things had suddenly taken a drastic turn, and it didn't look good.

I summoned a cab, bolting down the hall of the condo and out of the building to take a silent and terrifying ride to the hospital. Could this be it? Is this the end? Upon arriving, I saw the man I'd loved for thirty years: an oxygen mask covering his face, the awful sounds of his moaning with laboured breathing and that God-Awful death rattle, his eyes shut, his system shutting down. Steve held on for almost another two hours before I told him, "You know, there are a lot of people who really love you." With that his breathing slowed and finally stopped.

Now I've got a ticket on a journey I didn't ask to take. The plans we made, the dreams we had… my life is now changed drastically and forever. This wasn't the way it was supposed to be. However, I have no regrets or guilt. Steve and I had thirty wonderful years together, and during his time in the hospital, I was there for him every day from early in the morning until late afternoon. I was front-and-centre for him, totally in each moment. I helped administer his injections, gave him bed baths, went on errands for him, and most importantly, I was there for him the whole time. And what I understand now is that in being present and strong for him, I was present and strong for me. I now understand I have strengths I never knew I even possessed.

I have looked to the sky and asked, "Why Steve? Why Us?" There are no answers, and it doesn't matter. These things are as they are. I accept this, and in accepting this, I've found the strength to face each day. I believe that my being by Steve's side and holding his hand while he passed has gone a long way in my acceptance (how could it not?) Through this acceptance, I have found the strength and courage to deal with it and carry on.

The thing about the passing of a long-term partner is, you know you're single now, your head has no problem wrapping itself around that fact. Your heart, however, does not feel that way. I miss Steve being physically here, especially the little things. I miss his touch, his kiss, holding him, spoiling him, the fun and the teasing. After thirty years of building a life together, it was gut-wrenching for me to have to dismantle it all, one piece at a time.

I first met him in 1983 and had noticed Steve right away. He was rooming with the fellow I was seeing at the time, and unbeknownst to me, while I was noticing Steve, he was noticing me. During the time I was with Steve's roommate, Steve and I had become friends. Fast forward to 1985, only about four months since his roommate and I had split permanently, when Steve and I got together. I'll never forget his reaction to my telling him I wanted to be with him.

"Me?" he giggled like he couldn't believe anybody would ever tell him such a thing.

"Yes, you," I said, smiling back at him. And that's how it all began. It just clicked, and there was no turning back.

In the time since Steve's passing, I have learned I am strongest, most present and conscious when I'm in the moment. It's when I allow myself to dwell in the past that I become mournful and sad, longing for the way things were, as opposed to accepting the way things are. And yet, in spite of all that, I still have many moments where emotion gets the better of me: a song on the radio, finding an old photo, or the most emotional experience, finding cards with messages of love he had written to me years before. The cards may be old but reading them again feels like he's saying those things to me once again, like a message I need to hear.

Steve's passing was only the beginning of the many drastic changes in my life, and it hasn't even been a year since he's passed. The changes seem to piggyback each other, and mostly they're changes from within.

I've thought about it a lot, and if indeed the reason we are living our lives is to learn something, I've wondered if I'm here to learn inner strength? Why else would I choose to be a gay man in an age where I've witnessed the fear of AIDS right from the very genesis of the epidemic in the early eighties? I've watched so many people my own age wither away in front of me. Where the very lives of our community were nothing more than a game of political hot potato, musical chairs, moralising and finger-pointing over which point of view was the most righteous while hundreds of thousands got sick and died. Why else would I choose a relationship where the man I love, a healthy, vibrant, creative and active man, suddenly becomes ill and passes away?

On the other hand, maybe we're just all here to experience the full range of emotions and experiences that life has in store, the joyful and painful. After all, those experiences are the things we take with us when it's our turn to pass. Our money stays here, our religion, our politics, hell, even the things we paint, write, photograph, and create in general all get left behind. And will any of them matter in the future? Who knows?

And then there was the night of The Blood Moon.

September 27, 2015. That night shone a full moon--a Blood Moon they call it, because it appears red in the sky. Now add the fact that it was a lunar eclipse, so the energy was rare, and because of that something incredible happened that night while I was at work.

I was just leaving the staff lunchroom to walk down a hallway toward the staff washroom, which was by the back entrance to the Bloedel Conservatory in Queen Elizabeth Park in Vancouver. I was alone, yet while I walked I felt a hand slip into my left hand. I knew it, was Steve. I could feel his presence around me, and I could physically feel his hand in mine. It felt wonderful and reassuring.

I continued to walk down the hallway to the area where the food for the birds in the Conservatory was prepared every day. It's a small yet open area with a door out to the main area of the Conservatory, and almost opposite to it, there is a small staircase leading eight steps down to the boiler room and the staff washroom. On the left side of that staircase is a narrow ramp.

As I went down the stairs, I could feel Steve descend the ramp beside me and, still feeling my hand in his, my hand followed his upward while he was playfully teasing. As we went into the boiler room, I felt his hand move out of mine, and I felt his arm around my waist. It felt absolutely real to me.

I was filled with so much emotion at that moment that I could hardly express my elation. I cried. I said, "I love you, Steve," and I heard him say, "I love you too dear," in that special little way he would always say it to me.

I thought about it while on my way home that night. It was appropriate that this incident should happen while I was working at the Bloedel Conservatory. After all, it was where Steve served his apprenticeship for the Vancouver Parks Board. And it was where he spent the last twelve years of his working career as a gardener before he retired in 2013. The great patch of ground he tilled and planted was all around the outside of the Conservatory and sloped down a hill from there. I began working at the conservatory during the final year he worked there. He was on the outside during the day, and I worked on the inside during the late afternoon and evening.

That night, just as I was drifting to sleep, I saw myself climbing a grassy hill, and as I came to the top I saw Steve standing in a small field with our beloved cat Bennie in his arms. He smiled at me as I hurried over to him. I put my arms around the two of them, and again I cried as I felt Steve put his head on my shoulder and I heard Bennie purring.

One thing is for sure, that night at work during the Blood Moon changed everything. It demonstrated that I am indeed not alone, I am still loved, and most of all, everything is okay. I'll be fine no matter what happens.

Somewhere there's a field
And when I finally cross over
Steve will meet me there
With our beloved cat Bennie
And we'll celebrate together.

S.R.M. Duff

S.R.M. Duff lives in Victoria, Canada, with his cat, Bagheera (Bags). He has always been a curious observer of human nature and enjoys laughing at life's little absurdities. "Not a Love Story" is his first published short story.

Not A Love Story

As he walked along the path up and out of the valley, he could still smell the smoke of the burning forest behind him; he could still feel the sting from the smoke in the back of his dry throat. His pain remained constant as he limped along the path. All was silent except for his ragged breathing, his pounding heartbeat, and the sound of his footsteps along the dirt path. The silence was almost maddening.

Suddenly a shadow darted out in front of him and blocked his path as an 8-foot-tall monster. "Seriously?" he grunted, "I don't have time to dance with my demons; leave me be." The shadow split into two more figures and began to take form as his past loves, to torment and wound him further. One shadow took form as his first love; the second took form as his last love. "This is new," he chuckled. "Demonised versions of past loves? Normally it's just versions of me." As the final shadow took form as his true love, he clenched his fists and began to shake with rage. "NO!" he screamed, boiling with pure rage, his eyes welling up. "You have no right to demonise her! She doesn't deserve that, get out of my head!" He wanted to fight, but he was too tired. "Leave me alone!"

His first love sprang forward and sank a shadowy meat hook on a chain into his left shoulder. He screamed in agony as he wrapped his arm around the chain to lessen the pain. The ground behind them split open to a pit of dark despair. "No, I'm not going back there!" As he began to pull on the chain, trying to get away from his demons, his last love, the true evil, lunged forward and sank another hook into him, dropping him to his knees. The demon wrapped the chain around his neck and began to strangle him. He locked eyes with the demon in the form of his true love, and, gasping for air, he began to remember the warmth of her love, the real her. He closed his eyes, remembering happy memories, and felt a ray of loving white light take shape in his chest. He pushed it out of his body and roared as the white light erupted from his body like an explosion and disintegrated the shadows of his mind.

Freed from the chains for the moment, he continued out of the valley. As he reached the top of the valley, he turned to stare back down at the ruins below, the smoke still billowing up into the crisp early-morning sky. The sun had yet to crest the mountain range, but the sky was beginning to lighten. He pulled the mask covering his face down around his neck and let the cool breeze caress his hot and damp skin. The weight of his body armour began to feel too heavy as he started searching for a place to rest. He decided on a huge oak tree and collapsed beneath it. Resting with his back against the oak, he lifted his hands, rested them on his knees, palms up, and examined them. They were covered in dirt, soot, and even a bit of his own blood. He brought his hands shakily up to cover his face as he began to weep.

"Silly boy," he heard a voice--her voice--call to him. "What's the matter?" He turned his head to face her, and there she stood like an angel, an apparition, she smiled at him with that warm, loving smile of hers. It was his greatest love, his beautiful girl. What she must think seeing him in this state! Why would she be here: after all the pain she caused him, could she really care? She walked closer and knelt next to him. "I know you're hurting, and I'm sorry." She brought her hand up to wipe away his tears, still streaming down his dirty face, but he pushed her hand away.

"You have nothing to be sorry about," he said as he began to stand up. "We both knew this would be the outcome," he groaned from the effort of standing, as he unzipped his body armour and let it drop to the ground with a thud. The plates in it were too heavy now; he could not think clearly. His shirt was matted to his back from the sweat; it felt good to feel the breeze.

"I thought I was the love of your life," she said, the smile now completely gone from her face replaced with a look of concern and worry. "Am I no longer welcome here?"

"Of course you are, girl, this is my Shangri-la, you're always welcome, but shouldn't you be with your new love?" he replied.

"Yes, but I just wanted to speak with you. I know you're hurt, but I want you to be okay," she said. "I know you will be. You're strong." He let out a heavy sigh and wiped his face with his dirty hands.

"Yeah, strong... that may be true, but even the very strong need time to rest. After such heartbreak, my strength comes and goes." He turned to face her, looking into those big beautiful eyes he fell in love with. "I just want you to be happy, but I want to be with you."

"I know," she said, "but I'm happier with him. He's like my shining star, like a light at the end of the tunnel, like…"

"I KNOW," he roared. "I know, I get it," he whispered. "But not all lights at the end of the tunnel are good, they can be oncoming trains," he said with his voice breaking; "and stars don't last forever, but your decisions are yours to make. Good or bad, I'll support you." He could see her eyes welling up. "I love you, baby; I want you to be happy." He reached for her hands and held them tightly. "But your path with this guy is one I can't go down with you. No, I'm not saying I'll leave you, nor am I saying it's him or me. You've already made that choice." He could feel himself begin to cry again. "It's doubtful we can be friends when I'm still in love with you."

"I know," she whispered, "but he's different, maybe..."

"No, sweetheart," he said. "It's just disrespectful of me to strain your relationship with someone that makes you so happy." He let go of her hands. "Don't you think I feel the same about you as you do him?" He took a few steps back from her, "You say you know my pain, but how can you stand there and expect me to believe that?" He began to raise his voice even as it trembled, "I am not going to tell you your own feelings, but did you ever really love me? Do you even really care?"

She rolled her eyes and let out an exhausted sigh. "I hate having to repeat myself, we have been over this a million times, boy." She became more and more agitated. "Yes, I DID love you, but not as much as you love me. I do care; you are my friend."

"BUT I LOVE YOU!" he yelled. "Yes, we had trouble, yes, I didn't treat you right from day one, but we have a history. We shouldn't just give up on something that was so good."

Tears came streaming down her face as she spoke. "I gave up on us a long time ago. I wasn't happy, but now I am, and I'm not putting my happiness on hold for someone else. Don't you want to see me happy?"

He let out another heavy sigh and whispered, "I know baby, I know, and I admire you for that. Of course, I want you to be happy, and I know you want me to be happy too. I guess I'm just dragging my heels."

She turned to look down at the smouldering valley. "Is that because of me?" she asked. He glanced down at the valley too.

"No, been like that for years," he said, becoming aware of his aching body again, "but that on the other hand is all you." He gestured to the ruins of what looked like a temple, with what once was a raging bonfire now reduced to a small flame. "That is the fire of your love that burns in my heart, and I will never let it go out." A smile crept across her face again as she looked up at him. He met her gaze and said, "Whatever happens, you know where to find me, my love." He tapped his fist against his chest. "This sheepdog will always look after his sheep." She wrapped her arms around him, and they embraced. "It's all just in my head, I'll be fine, don't worry," he said.

"I'm still going to worry," she whispered, "you're still important to me." She placed a kiss on his cheek, and he placed one on her forehead. "Be good," she whispered tenderly in his ear, as she let go of him. They held hands for a moment before she turned and headed into the forest that surrounded the valley.

"You're always welcome here, my love," he called after her. "It doesn't matter how high these mountains or the walls I build are; you'll always find a way in anyway." She turned her head and looked over her shoulder as she continued to walk away.

"Yeah ,pretty much," she chuckled, "It's not Hawaii, but it will do. Go on, go fight your demons; I believe in you. I'll always be there to help you," she called.

He turned back to face the valley after watching her disappear into the woods. The sun had finally crested the mountains, and he closed his eyes and breathed in the sunlight. He heard an eagle cry, and he opened his eyes to see it circling the valley. He smiled, looked around the valley, and saw the green returning. He picked up his armour. He still felt empty; he still missed his love; but with the breaking of dawn and a new day rising, he felt... ready, ready to plow the earth and start again. He may never love another, he may never be with her again, but he felt the strength of the universe and the love of Mother Nature beckon to him.

Donning his armour once more, he smirked "Well, I have a lot of work to do. Maybe she'll find a reason to return to me once I fix this, or maybe I will find my purpose." He began walking back down the path, illuminated in the sun's bright and warm light. He whispered her name into the wind, and a ray of light manifested into a sword, one he could use to fight with and cut the lies his demons created.. He picked it up and felt her love and the love of his family and friends surge through him, and he knew it would guide him. He continued down the path, with hope, faith, and the determination to rebuild all that had been wrecked over time by the evil of the world and by his own mind.

The valley, his valley, was what he saw with his third eye. His ageless hiding place, where he can seek haven from the hardships of life. He vowed not to let the wrong people do him harm any longer. Whether he ultimately gave up on love or not did not matter. What did matter for him at that moment was being at peace with himself.

That is a long road that we all must walk one day; one we never truly walk alone.

The End... for now.

Thomas Keesman

Thomas Keesman continues to be the unstoppable reader he became on opening his first book. At 12, he decided to write science fiction. Now retired from public service, he is finally pursuing that five-decade-old goal with "unseemly enthusiasm".

Keesman draws on life, historical events, and an overactive sense of "so, what if..." His stories often explore how individuals at the margins of society cope with the challenges of both daily life and extraordinary change.

He has a self-published novel *Extraordinaire,* (2013). Short stories in The Unvalentine Anthology (Filidh 2015). His current projects include two collections of short stories, a novella and a prequel to *Extraordinaire*. Keesman was born in Victoria, Canada–where he still lives, loves, and writes in the company of family and Fergus the Bad Cat.

A Republic Of Dogs

If you were to ponder the collective lives of free canines, where would they be? No, don't answer. This is my story, so I get to tell you. But Kant or some other dead German said something about needing to know where you are before you can ponder where anything else is. Maybe it was some dead French guy. Doesn't matter. I will begin by telling you where I am.

I am sitting in the exact centre of the Kingdom of Gary. The centre moves too, depending on where I put the old wooden stool that serves as my Chair of State. Sometimes it ends up with a view of Third Street. Not much happens there, except the time huge old Opa Mueller across the street got stuck in the tub. They called the fire department to get him out, but that wasn't so interesting really. The best view is when I drag the stool to the window so I can look at the apple tree.

It is a good place, as it is where I used to sit in the shade with Cherise's head on my lap, her tail wagging as I tried to read books out loud. Most were pretty hard, but we both really liked a book that Father had when he was little. It was the story of Mike Mulligan and Mary Anne. We liked the part where they found a place they could stay, and everyone welcomed them. There were lots of pictures that made the story better.

We read or played whenever we wanted because a special exemption form said I didn't have to go to regular school. I attended Friskar Elementary for thirteen days until the teacher's union filed a claim of undue and unusual stress. I read their submission on the secure internet site,

160

which was almost too easy to break into. All the names were blacked out, but I knew who was who. If Mrs. [name blacked out] broke down like that, I really hope the school board does a better job now of screening who gets to be a student. Anyway, I was homeschooled under the supervision of a visiting tutor. No one ever showed up, and none of the adults said anything. I didn't either.

I want you to know that the Chair of State is my chair, and it moves whenever I want it to. It also might help you to know the Kingdom of Gary is what the *mal- imaginative* think is just the attic of Grandmother's house. I just made that word up. It's pretty neat. Maybe I can use it at dinner tonight. Maybe not. But it is a good word. And a good chair. I was sitting on it twenty-nine years ago when I heard about the dog republic. And the reason I was even interested in it was because, three months earlier, Cherise was let out the back door to go pee. She never came back.

Just ninety-one days later I found out where she went, thanks to Mrs. Doris Marie Hundre and KSJR-AM. She told the whole story, all in one go. I never met her, but that is not surprising. She lives down south, some place on San Francisco Bay. It is the same place that KSJR lived too.

I always liked the radio. When I couldn't sleep, I went to the attic and tuned into stations all around the world, all through the night. One night, I started DXing at the bottom of the dial but didn't find anything better than a boring beatnik talk show from the Portland College of Communications. So I moved up to the top end of the dial half an hour before sunrise. You get the best signals at sunset and sunrise. That morning I found a station I never heard before–KSJR, on the AM dial. I missed the broadcast power, but it wasn't more than fifty watts. If that.

I missed a bunch of stuff because of static, then a lot more because Mrs. Doris Marie Hundre was kind of sobbing and sighing when host Chuck Thaw clicked her live on the air. When she went live, oh my goodness! It was as if she was puking out her words all at once. I was getting ready to dial down when she said her lovely little poodle had abandoned the comforts of life in the Hundre house for FREEDOM ON FOREIGN SHORES! Mrs Hundre didn't say it was all capitals with an exclamation mark, but I heard them. I am sure every other listener of KSJR also heard them.

Mr. Thaw faded her out, then said, "Chuck Thaw here with a great big KSJR good morning to all our listeners around the Bay. KSJR, the station at the top of everybody's dial! Today we're talking about where runaway dogs go." He cut back to Mrs. Hundre on the telephone. The sound was really bad. I think her telephone was about the last rotary handset still used in the entire state of North California.

The month before, she said, she was crying to a friend about her dog running away. After an hour on the telephone, the friend said to meet her at the local HaidaBucks (back then it was a new coffee chain with an Alaskan Native theme. Now EVERYONE has their own HaidaMug. Even me). Once there, as Mrs. Doris Marie Hundre repeated her story, an old man at the next table joined in.

His little Fifi had run off the year before. When he told his cousin, a driver for South California DOT in Pasadena, the cousin got all quiet. The cousin said he knew where Fifi and a whole lot of other missing dogs went. But don't worry. It was a good story.

The cousin got it from a fellow he worked with. That man's daughter's best friend's half-sister had it first hand from an Animal Control Officer she was dating in Vancouver, British Columbia, Canada. A lot of people knew about this, but none of them really talked about it. Many didn't because they couldn't believe it themselves. Some, because they didn't want to be called liars. Others thought dogs deserved to make their own choices and to be free if they wanted. Here's how the story went.

Years ago, there was a lab cross named Trixie, who belonged to an inventor from Santa Clara. He was already rich from selling a shelf-lined gate to NM Electrics. None of this makes any sense to me, but the electric guys must have liked whatever it was. They gave him a lot of money. Anyway, Trixie had a radio transmitter on her collar because her owner was making some kind of mathematical map of daily dog routines. One day, when she was let out the back door, she ran straight to the back fence, then back to the house. She jumped up and down a couple of times then ran to the back and zoomed right over the fence. All before the inventor's eyes.

He watched a little radar screen to track Trixie up the Valley, then lost her. But the inventor was determined to follow the trail. If for no other reason than he wanted his radio back. I wish he wanted Trixie back more, but "some people", as Mother used to say.

The inventor called his brother, also an inventor guy, and together they drove up the I-5 towards Walnut Creek then Vallejo. This was really strange, because it meant Trixie was running at nearly 40 miles per hour. The signal kept going north. So on they went to Redding, then Portland and Seattle. By then, they figured Trixie was in a car or something. Ha! I got that right away. Boy, they thought, someone must really really want Trixie, to dognap her and bring her all the way to the shadow of the Space Needle. I went to the top once, but the rotating restaurant made me motion sick. I threw up on my sister's shoes. The beeping signal kept leading them even more north.

It was just after midnight when they arrived at the border with Canada. The signal was getting faint because the battery was running out–then it died. The border guard (who didn't even have a gun) asked what their business in Canada was. They didn't know what to say, so they accidentally told the truth. We're looking for a stolen dog, they said. But we don't know where she is now because the battery died.

The border guard was confused until they explained that the radio battery that died, not the battery for the dog. He called the Metropolitan Vancouver Animal Control Office for advice. But between eleven p.m. and six a.m., callers only got an answering service. Even as the gunless border guard was explaining that to the brothers, his telephone rang. It was the on-call animal control officer. He was finishing up a call nearby and could help them right away.

The border guard looked surprised, then asked how far away he might be. The ACO (they like being called that instead of dog catcher) told the guard to look over at the groundskeeping shed across the parking lot. He did, and a man in an ACO uniform was standing with a cellular telephone to his ear. He waved at the border guard, and they both laughed. I guess Canadians do that kind of thing all the time.

The ACO was there because of a complaint about an owl swooping at night shift workers around the Peace Arch border crossing. He walked across the lot and listened to the inventor brothers' story. After following the radio signal for nearly a week, the brothers were starting to feel like it was a foolish mission. They were embarrassed, and kind of hoped the ACO would just tell them to go home.

Instead, he took them to an all night cafe, where he told a tale of his own, drew a map, then sent them on their way. He said they would get there about dawn and have to wait for the first fairy. The inventor brothers drove through miles of flat farmland before getting to the actual city of Vancouver, British Columbia, Canada. Then they drove through the city, over the Lion Skate Bridge, and up to Horseshoe Landing. Someplace along there, the driving brother said they'd clocked a thousand miles. Because they were far north of San Francisco, and it was early morning, it was cold, but not Canada cold. They didn't even see any Royal Canadian Mounties with dogsleds, which surprised me as much as it had the old man telling the story. By then, Mrs. Hundre's friend remembered an important appointment and hurried off.

The brothers waited for a ferry boat, which makes more sense than some sort of pixie. Then they drove for a while until they reached a village called Sechelt. (Do you think Canadian places have funny names too?) Just before getting

165

to the business strip, the map said to turn right, drive two miles, then take the left fork past the bridge. They were supposed to go to the turn-around, then walk the rest of the way. The narrow lane had grass growing down the middle. Sure enough, it ended in a wide turn-around, surrounded by a circle of mossy concrete blocks.

A million years or so ago, glaciers dumped a bunch of gravel there. When I was ten, I thought it would be like a dog taking a poop. That's not right, but I still don't know how or why the glaciers brought all that gravel there. Anyway, people started digging the gravel up and turning it into sidewalks and skyscrapers and stadiums. When they were done, the people moved on, leaving big holes of nothing much.

The inventor brothers walked past the blocks and crawled through a broken wire fence to stand at the edge of a used-up gravel pit. There were no dogs, just rocks and clay and bunches of little stick trees. They walked around trying to figure out what to do next when a little man with a big voice yelled right behind them. "Go away! Private property! Nothing to see here!" He looked them up and down before adding, "Go away!"

The inventor brothers said they were just looking for their dog. The old man got even madder. "No dogs here! Go away!" The men looking past him to a grey poodle peeking out through a piece of plastic draped over a bush. "Ignore that dog behind the shower curtain! Go away!"

"Is that your dog?" they asked. He shouted some more, telling them no one owned dogs in this place. They were free dogs, who ran their own lives in A REPUBLIC OF

DOGS. Holy cow, that was the very first time I heard those words said out loud. The man lived at the edge of the pit and never got mad at the dogs there or tried to make them do things his way. They never tried to make him act like a dog. Everybody just worked at getting along.

The brothers apologised, and asked him to tell them about it. Once they promised to leave afterwards, he said there were about two hundred dogs of all sorts there. Some were Canadian, most American, with a few Mexican dogs. When one brother asked how he knew, the old man shook his head at their foolish youth. He said when they barked, their accents gave them away, clear as day.

He talked about how they lived free, and never even chased stray cats who came through. The inventor brothers said that was very interesting. So maybe Trixie was better off here. But they were sad not to at least get the collar back. The old hermit man growled almost like a dog, then stomped off into the bush. In two minutes, he came back to throw the radio collar at them. "There's your damn collar. Go away." They did. It sounds like they stopped to tell the friendly ACO what happened, but no one else. Still, word eventually got around to the man who lost his Fifi.

Mrs. Hundre started to say how the old man said runaway dogs from as far away as San Diego would sneak onto northbound trucks or trains or even buses (Greyhounds! Did you guess?) to get to Seattle. Local dogs would help guide them on their journey. Then... then she started getting fuzzy. There was a lot of random noise, followed by steady static. The sun was full up. The atmospheric layers were back to doing what they were supposed to be doing. Regular daytime signals drowned out small, far away stations. The Chuck Thaw Show was gone.

I tried for weeks to find KSJR again. I went to the library and read all the pages in the Southwest States section of the Green Book of Radio Communications in America. I even looked at all the phone books for Greater San Francisco. KSJR was nowhere to be found.

The reference librarian, Mrs. Sprague, was always helpful and nice to me. She wondered if the call letters might be something to do with San Jose, which was a little town swallowed up by the City of Milpitas—you know, like the Carpenter's song "Do You Know the Way to Milpitas Bay?"

I sent tonnes of postcards to their city hall, the Chamber of Commerce, the BBB, the Elks and Lions and Optimists, the Broadcasting Alliance of the Californias, Santa Clara County offices, even the local Boy Scouts (because my cousin Little Ed had a BSA Radioman badge on his sash). Mrs. Sprague suggested sending one to KSJR with only the name and city. That was technically an incomplete address (and against postal regulations), but she said it worked sometimes. So I tried. It didn't work. I got five responses from all my postcards. Three were pre-printed thank-you letters, with brochures. The others suggested I contact the Broadcasting Alliance. Nothing from, or about, KSJR.

That was years and years ago. I am now forty-two and have bad eyes and diabetes, and my sister says I am way, way overweight—maybe bigger than Mr. Mueller even. I still have my little room on the third floor and the attic above it. I hope you are as pleased as I am that the Kingdom of Gary still "stands on guard for thee-ee". I borrowed that last part from the Canada anthem in honour of the Republic of Dogs.

Grandmother died, then Father and Mother died, and then the house and I went to my sister Geraldine. Sometimes, she gets mad at me. That is OK, though. She can't get mad at her husband, because when he drinks, he says awful things (and he mostly drinks all the time). She can't get mad at Brian Jr. because he is in danger of self-harm. I don't know what that is, but it doesn't sound good. The two youngest children just keep their heads down. They are nice, and sometimes even say nice things about me. I once heard Gwen say to Connor to appreciate me because I was a lightening rod.

It's true. If Geraldine comes into a room ready to be mad, and her kids and I are there, she always scolds me. What Gwen didn't know is, it is better than when we were kids. Then, her mom would go weeks without ever saying a word to me. But it's not always easy when your sister talks to you, like when Geraldine came into my room the summer Mother died.

I was sitting on my bed looking at a photograph of Cherise and me taken on the back stairs. Geraldine got all red in her face when I said I wished I had another of Cherise up in Sechelt with her dog friends. She said she was sure Father hired voice actors to pretend-broadcast a big malarkey story about dogs running off to Canada. Just so I would stop thinking about, talking about, and pining for my damn runaway dog.

When Geraldine swore, I knew then and there she was wrong. Mother used to sit me down after every visit from her brother Edgar. Uncle Edgar swore a lot. Mother would say "Gary, swearing is never right." Geraldine swore, and swearing is wrong. That makes Geraldine wrong. That makes the Dog Republic real.

**

Today, the mailman came by with four letters. Two were bills for Brian Senior. One was a letter to Gwen from her pen pal in Ireland. The last one was in a light blue envelope with a return address from San Francisco. For me. From Mrs. Sprague, the nice reference librarian.

She and Mr. Sprague moved back to San Francisco when they retired. Mr. Sprague is on the board of the Castro Community Center, and Mrs. Sprague is working on a book about the redevelopment of the old Delores Airfield. In her searches of metro area newspapers, she found Chuck Thaw! What she found was a death thing--an obit, she called it-- from 1983, which was the year I heard the story of a republic of dogs. He died when a semi loaded with lumber rammed three cars at a freeway exit in Oakland. She quoted from another article called "Tanker Tragedy Claims Two":

"Carlos Vernon Taugh had achieved his lifelong ambition to start his own radio station only a few days before the tragic event. Taugh was the owner, general manager, and morning host for the provisionally licenced KXAR. His death, and that of his son, the station's audio technician, meant KXAR signed off forever that day. Maureen Taugh told reporters her husband had followed his dream, and now the dream must follow him. Taugh was best known for his failed campaign to prevent Milpitas, South Bay's powerhouse from annexing tiny San Jose ..."

Mrs. Sprague hoped that this was helpful, and that I was well. She didn't ask me to write her back. That was OK.

So, now you know where this started, and you too can ponder if my little Cherise got to Sechelt, and maybe found what she was looking for. Doesn't matter what you think, because I know she did.

Whenever I walk to the barber or the 7-Eleven, Geraldine sends one of the younger children along to make sure I don't wander or pester people. If I see a Greyhound bus go by, I salute it. The kids used to get embarrassed when I did. Now, most of the time, Connor joins me. I bet Cherise would give a happy bark.

THE END

The Great Seattle Progress of 1874

PART 1: Incidental Conversations

On April 1, 1868, many Americans suspected a prank on reading that their nation had grown by 6,300 square miles overnight. That changed to surprise on confirmation that the Hudson's Bay Company ceded its Puget Sound Settlement (PSS) to the United States for something less than fifteen cents an acre.

It was not a surprise to everyone's taste, though. The American press dubbed the $600,000 cost "Seward's Folly". The Secretary of State endured a nasty Congressional inquiry, just avoided censure, then finally resigned in disgust and exhaustion. But they didn't hang him. The Company's board was less fortunate. Transported in chains to the infamous Isle of Man prisons, most were, in fact, hung.

Still in shock, a few hundred loyalist Britons prepared to flee north to British Columbia. The last Company man ashore, a junior clerk, unceremoniously hauled down the Union Jack just before boarding the waiting steamer. At the foot of the gangplank, his coat pocket jingled: a ring of warehouse, office and jail keys. Shrugging, he tossed the key ring toward the foot of the naked flagpole. As many aboard gazed back for a final look at the lost colony, the clerk bent over a diary to note the disposal of the keys. Half an hour later, the eight-gun USS Beaver docked, bearing the temporary Federal governor and a fifty-man garrison for the new American territory.

The former PSS was straightaway incorporated into Washington Territory and divided into three new counties.

One was later renamed in honour of the departed temporary governor,. Edwin DeVane King. The famous nephew of a largely forgotten vice president, he remained in place for little more than three months. His farewell speech was peppered with predictions of Seattle's greatness as the sea, rail, and air hub of the Northwest.

The change of ownership sparked a buying and building frenzy. Money and settlers poured in; a naval station and an army base were established; a commercial airfield opened three miles from the city. The county commissioners ignored grumbles about the distance. The deadly explosive potential of hydrogen was fresh in many minds, including those of two commissioners who survived the Baltimore disaster three years earlier.

With greatness just around the corner, a syndicate assembled an American version of a Hallistone Machine. Sitting among compressed air pistons and drive chains, the Machine powered a host of digging and levelling, earthmoving and pile-driving, mortar-pumping and brick-laying devices. Locals flocked to point in wonder at the speed and sureness with which millions of bricks were laid to become the central rail station, maintenance sheds, water towers and warehouses, commercial blocks, paved streets, tunnels, and viaducts.

The Victoria Evening Telegraph choked back a measure of patriotic envy long enough to admit "the work of this modern mechanical marvel will secure Seattle's place in the hearts and minds of all Americans on the west coast. Discerning Britons will understand that notice has been served in the North Pacific."

Of course, all this was true only when the Machine was working. By May of 1874, the Hallistone's devices had been motionless for nearly six weeks. A defect in the monster steam engine that powered the various activities rendered the construction precinct silent, all but abandoned.

As the flow of money dwindled, suppliers and builders and three-dollar-a-week labourers became restive. The governor and his treasurer discussed new public work projects to absorb some of the unemployed. He also quietly consulted with the colonel of the territorial militia about the possibility of general civil disorder. The arrival in Elliott Bay of the steamer carrying the replacement engine rendered a declaration of martial law unnecessary.

In the weeks prior to the arrival of the replacement, sharper minds recognised the real delay would occur after the ship docked. The original machine had been dragged in during high summer, after months of preparing a skid causeway to the site, and routed through empty lands.

Now stretches of still-settling fill, winter rain ponds, permanent marshes, mud-greased hills, and streets full of new construction lay between shore and site. It was thought a thousand horses and twice that many men would take twenty days to clear the way, then move the mass of iron. A quandary certainly, until an unnamed clerk jokingly suggested one modern marvel could move another.

Among the fleets moored at Union Bay Field, the Daphne lifted half again as much as the next largest airship. Boxwood and brass numerators slid and clacked to feed scores of pages of calculations. They found the Daphne provided insufficient lift. More clacking led to auxiliary balloons being attached to the engine's mass. When the Daphne was actually harnessed, the load came nearly a foot off the ground. Close, but not quite.

Why not one modern marvel towing another which was lifting the third? Off came the motors and the massive springs that powered them. The rear gondola was stripped of every non-structural part: bulkheads were knocked out, ports stripped of glass, and doors torn from hinges. Ballast tanks were emptied, then for good measure, cut off and added to the growing debris pile below. One spectator recalled to his grandchildren decades later that it was the most magnificent vandalism he had ever witnessed.

The estimate of five hours before another ship could be fitted for towing the Daphne swept through the gathered throngs. With the grand spectacle now deferred for half a day, the crowds sorted themselves into knots of conversation, card or dice play, and moody drinking.

As their impatient buzz took on an increasingly sullen tone, a number of capital "I". Important men gathered near the gutted Daphne. They glanced at each other, then gave their full attention to a large, bull-bodied man dressed in an outlandishly bright suit. He looked directly and deliberately into the face of each man before bowing his head briefly. Looking up, he spread his arms to make a gentle pulling motion, as if he were a referee bringing two pugilists in for the pre-fight talk. They closed in to stand nearly shoulder to shoulder. A ring of toughs insulated the Territory's preeminent capitalists from eavesdroppers and other pests.

Arthur Brickley rolled out quick, muted sentences. "Gentlemen, we all know the mischief a bored mob can get up to. A nicely organised riot can be a very good thing. But this does not have the air of a beneficial situation. The delay of the promised show has put them barely one step from serious mischief. I can turn them, but only with your help. If you're in, stay. Otherwise, good day." He gestured to one of the toughs, who came over for whispered instructions. When the man left, Brickley looked up. Most stayed for the practical reason that Brickley had a nose for the dollar. A couple stayed with the hope of seeing him fail. The lesser lights remained because leaving might be seen as disrespect for him--never a good idea. Brickley knew who was in each camp but ignored that in his drive for results.

"Right then. I am reminded of something Pa told me from the Old Country, just before he came over. Short of it is this. Pa built a balloon for a fellow for... for an adventure. This man, Poole, needed to move it quiet-like, but back then airships were moved by steam only. Poole had his own bullyboys to build it, then tow it by plain old main force. No idle minds, no idle bodies, see? It worked then. It can work for us."

Some caught his drift right away or pretended so. Others laboured along to calculate the unknown cost against the equally unknown potential. In the end, each signalled his moral and financial support.

A scant half hour later, every able-bodied male spectator within shouting distance was called to one of four marshalling points. There, speakers delivered a mix of revival-meeting catch phrases and native-son rhetoric. They also delivered the "two plus two" promise: two dollars a man and tokens for two free drinks at any establishment in the country. Following three cheers, they set about readying the impromptu work gangs for the task ahead.

As the speeches rolled out, so too did four giant hawsers attached to the Daphne's forward ring. The lines, long enough for three hundred hands to grip, were laid radiating out from the bow. Another trailed behind to provide a brake if needed. The first pistol shot prompted fifteen hundred men to lay hands on those lines. The second shot caused them to hoist lines to shoulders. The third shot signalled a slow walk forward.

Line scouts ran ahead, picking out the best routes along the maze of new streets. In a few instances the gangs, dragging through orchards, building sites, and a cemetery, caused considerable damage. The last of the resulting suits was settled in territorial courts just before Washington gained statehood fifteen years later.

Those not bearing a hand stood along the way, cheering, shouting advice, or simply gawking. Some hawked cold drinks and hot snacks, or seats to the best viewpoints of what was being dubbed "The Great Seattle Progress." The best views were from the city's numerous hilltops.

Arthur Brickley and two of his partners climbed Queen Anne Hill to stand in front of Sal's, one of the better sporting houses built during the British era. When the Company vacated, Sally Sharpe stayed on. Brickley was fond of saying that while her looks were long dulled, her tongue and temper still lived up to the name.

As if his thoughts were a summons, Sally appeared carrying a bottle in one hand and a stack of glasses in the other. She poured a round, including a generous measure for herself. The four stood sipping and admiring the panorama before them. Brickley eyed her with caution. There was a mercenary purpose in Sally's every act, even when only providing a courtesy drink. Especially then.

"Lord, what a sight. Takes me back to me girlhood. I'se entertaining an over-nighter, and during a rest, I looks out the window. A great bag of canvas and rags, trailing ropes like jellyfish legs, floated right on by. A host of ruffians hung off'en them ropes. A couple of regulars waved friendly-like. Not a word was said while they drifted down the street, just so ghosty. Aye, an' still a wonder after all these years."

The three men looked at her, then at each other, unable to find the connection between her tale and the airship below with the hundreds pulling it along. She saw the looks and added, "What reminds me is that balloon was being towed by a gang, just the way this one is. Not nearly so many. Maybe forty thereabouts, I recollect. Seems they was off to yaffle a neighbouring rival. Might have done, but the army put the yaffle to both gangs. About then, it seemed best for me to set up in one of the colonies. And that's how I ended up here."

There was some general nodding among the men, and Sally subsided into silence. Then, with the faintest hint of malice, she spoke again. "You know, Arthur, next week the Governor be holding a levee of sorts for investors up from the Californias. Lots of big names rubbing shoulders. You should come along. Mayhap even meet a nice gal to name your next airship after. I hear 'Lizzy Ann' is still available. Hee hee."

The partners carefully hid their smiles. Brickley's face reddened at the mention of that particularly sore spot. Recently, a young woman of substantial family publicly scorned his private offer to christen an airship after her, ridiculing his well-known practice of "ride her, name her." Elizabeth Ann's brothers issued a standing challenge to him to settle this matter of family and feminine honour. Brickley could have easily taken them one at a time, or even as a group, but didn't want to alienate that family any further. He maintained an uncharacteristic silence to the challenge.

At this point, he also still valued the tidbits Sally regularly passed along. No sense in feuding with such a good source of gossip and hard intelligence. He offered a tight smile. With that neat twist of the knife, Sally felt vindicated for a recent cutting remark aimed at her from the Brick. Returning his smile, she gathered the glasses before disappearing inside. Leaning against the closed door, she smugly thought it had been well worth a dollar and a half in watered whiskey. Outside, Brickley spat.

The men turned back to watch the Great Progress again. The cargo floated a scant fifteen feet above the ground. It was enough. The tow gangs stumbled, laughing and shouting, over uneven terrain, around houses, wood piles, and everything else. By noon, the Daphne floated beside the sheet iron engine house in the centre of the moiling mud, rubble, and humanity of the vast construction site. A dozen piles of stacked corrugated iron sheets ringed the building, whose rafters had been unbolted and pushed to the middle and either end.

Since the payload could not be lifted higher, a section of the wall was hastily knocked out. The new engine was guided into one end of the shed. The Daphne was then pulled to the far end to carry away the defective member. When all was ready, another airship towed the Daphne and its iron tonnage to a bayside breaking yard.

Workmen began reassembling rafters and roof as soon as the new engine was in place. By the time the airship lifted the old engine, the new one was nearly covered over. Mechanical crews worked in a frenzy to put the engine in operation by noon the next day. The crowds dispersed. The taverns soon filled up and remained so until the early hours.

One bystander, who had ignored every invitation to join the work gangs, asked loudly why the hell they had exploited all those workingmen when they could have had another balloon haul the Daphne along in the first place. His nearest neighbour rounded on him, looking him up and down before speaking.

"You, sir, appear to be some sort of European. A Westphalian by accent, a bushman by dress, and a commu-anarchist by utterance. With all that baggage, I see how you were unable to apprehend the import of what just took place."

Taking part in the dragging of the airship was an investment by each and every man who was there, he declared. Now waving his arms about in the manner of old men relating epics of their youth, he said those men would tell and retell their part in moving the mass of iron and how they individually helped restart the engine that would build the heart and soul of their future metropolis.

"Why, it is just like the men who fought with Henry at Agincourt. You could take that speech of his, change the names, and it would be all the exact same, with some differences. But mostly the exact same."

He gestured to the empty space where the businessmen had met. "Those gentlemen may own the machines, and profit mightily from them. But today, a legend is born, and born well. How all these modern marvels depended on the good graces of that oldest and most honorable power source–the brawn and sinew of patient men of the soil and sea. Throughout the ages, it was such men as laboured to build Egyptian pyramids, Roman roads, and French canals.

"But this was a far greater achievement, as there were neither whips nor rods bending the workmen's backs. This will translate into a well-deserved celebration of the glory of the labour of free Americans–not slaves or convicts." He then heaped praise on every player in this epic, from the lowest water boy to the Daphne's gallant pilot.

The other shrugged. "Saxon, not Westphalian. Met that pilot, McCann. Little enough to meet the eye. Even less so when you get to know him."

But the other wasn't listening, having his teeth set to bone, as the saying goes. "Why, give 'em a role in a great enterprise, and that greatness reflects on them. Doing this multiplies the energy and dedication that would go into the common cause of a great and industrious America. Sir, today you have seen the greatness of the American republic in action. First, in the quite magnificent deed itself. Secondly, in the recounting that makes every American man proud and positive of his own worth and that of his nation." The man had run out of breath and words by that point. He stared, a bit bug-eyed, at the German.

"Humph. You might want to strain and bottle that spiel. You could pass it as genuine Canadian modesty, easy. Maybe get a nickel a bottle." The Saxon turned sharply on his heel to make his way through the thinning crowd.

With her appointed tasks complete, the Daphne was towed to her home port on Lake Washington. Once moored, the refit for general cargo and the reattachment of the motors began. The refit gang would work on the Daphne through to dawn.

The flight crew, bonuses in hand, would be busy through the night as well. They retired to a nearby hotel to celebrate in earnest. The next twelve hours were dedicated to food, drink, and other traditional pleasures of the flesh. None questioned their extra pay, despite the ground crews having controlled virtually everything about the move. But then, no man questions his own good fortune too closely.

By mid-morning, only one was still within bounds of the Caravan Hotel. As the first head of steam began building in the Hallistone's new boilers, the ill-spoken-of pilot laid into a late breakfast of a dozen oysters, with lubrication as needed. Outside, an Indian stood in the rain.

PART 2: *Accounts Payable*

Seattle can be disagreeably cold and wet in early May, even for those who have lived their whole lives there. That particular day was made no better for Samuel Luke by two hours waiting outside for the pilot to emerge. The hotel manager refused to disturb his guest, then denied Samuel the shelter of the Caravan's covered porch.

Emerging from the bar, Tobias McCann neither noticed or cared. He was still basking in the glow of a job well done, a substantial bonus (somehow all spent), and the bonhomie of celebration. Standing under cover, McCann belched discretely into his fur collar. A man has to have standards.

"Well, well, if it ain't Sammy the Seattle Siwash." He chuckled at his own wit. "Whatcha want, Sammy?"

"Boss Brickley, he want big talk talk with you. Say it past time to settle accounts for last year."

That got the pilot's attention. He blinked, shook his head to clear the bourbon chasers to those oysters. "Wha for?"

"He just say tell you. I hear Boss Brickley say to Mr. Killip he should be happy, as time overdue for payback. Killip smiled. That all. You give me quint for tell you?"

The shaken McCann flipped a twenty-cent coin to the Indian as he turned away. It fell in the mud. Holy shite, the Brick must have got wind of the guns he had run up to the Chilcoten. That Henderson bastard in Victoria must have peached him. The Brits fussed awful when folks sold guns to their Indians. Especially if those redskins were shooting at the red coats. Redskins, red coats, red-ass baboons. He giggled. Damn, he was the funniest man he ever knew.

McCann didn't give a tinker's dam for the Brits, and even less for their flea-bitten aborigines. On that run he hadn't seen anyone but a bunch of pissant Kraut communards fighting on the native side. The pilot bridled at the recollection. The head Kraut--Kray or May, or Ney, whatever--had promised gold francs. Instead, the Germans arrived with bags of mixed Mexican, Bolivian, and Argentine silver coins.

In the face of the pilot's outrage, all Herr Krautmeister had said was "Comes out to the same dollar value." McCann nearly left, but would then be forced to sell off a cargo of illegal guns. The Krauts probably counted on that. The pilot had contemplated a lightning run to Williams Lake to tip the British agent as to where the Indians were hiding. But he figured Henderson would have arrested him, then chased down the insurgents. So McCann had accepted the substitution with all the bad grace he could muster.

He had insisted they count out each bag, to the annoyance of both Germans and airship crew. Two acrimonious hours later, he agreed to offload the rifles. He had lifted the airship four feet before ordering the cargo pushed out the port. McCann had been altogether pleased with the sound of crates breaking and the rebel curses that followed. Irritation aside, after expenses, he had cleared a tidy seventy-five hundred. That was all spent though, far faster than he thought possible.

None of this would matter to his employer, other than the delivery being made with a Brickley airship. The Emma had supposedly been laid up with motor problems in Boise those two days. God knows, the Brick was no stranger to shady deals, but he insisted on his full cut. If his rightful share was not forthcoming, the man had a reputation for making cuts of his own. Personally. Painfully. As only someone who grew up rough in the San Diego docklands could. All this ran through McCann's mind in seconds, as he stood mute on the plank walk. Samuel was still bending over to fetch the silver piece.

"Why'd he send you, Sammy?"

"Not so many of us at the hanger this morning, Mr. McCann. Boss Brickley says I only one that know you by sight and have best English too. He must want you to know exactly what's coming. And just so you know, my name is not Sammy. It is Samuel Luke, for the prophet in the Old Book and the apostle of the New Book. I am baptised into the true faith."

McCann mumbled, "Yeah, that's something to be proud of, Sammy. Look me up if you ever get to au Mexique." It didn't occur to him that letting slip his destination was a bad idea. Indians didn't understand shit. And no one listened to them anyway. Without another word, he turned and scuttled along the wooden sidewalk, bound for the far side of the airfield.

McCann had already plotted his escape route--down the street, behind the passenger terminal, swapping out his clothes before making his way incognito to one of the North-South shipping concerns. Once there, he would hitch a ride to Los Angeles, then on to Mexico City. That should be far enough if he changed his name and stayed away from gasbags for a couple of years. He rounded the distant corner, with a final look behind to make sure no one was watching. Just the Indian. Safe.

Since joining Brickley Inland Air three years previously, the former Union air officer had treated Samuel with contempt in every possible way. His contempt was not exclusive to the Indian, but Samuel bore more of it, and more patiently, than any of the others. Until late in the autumn, when the pilot had accosted him at the rough market on the hill overlooking Elliott Bay. McCann had been, as usual, very drunk. He had also been in a funk over his banishment from Chinatown.

"Imagine Sammy, them John Chinamans saying it's not proper for me to stroll their filthy little alleys. Or sit in one of their cockroach diners." Finally, he had gotten to what was really bothering him. "Or spend my hard-earned cash money on their whores. The whores don't care. I don't care. Why should their owners care if I like things a little different?"

McCann had stared owl-eyed at Samuel in the timeless manner of perplexed drunks striving to impress on others how reasonable and aggrieved they are. Samuel had stood silently throughout the meandering whine. The pilot's face had brightened with inspiration.

McCann had leaned closer to ask with exaggerated dignity if Samuel might have a very young sister available. Or know someone who did. Young because he found floppy titties and fluff just plain disgusting. A man has to have standards. Regardless of the laws against trading alcohol to Indians, the pilot had promised to provide a whole bottle if

186

Sammy could help out old friend Tobias. In a gesture of sincerity, McCann took his hand in a sweaty grip. Samuel had feigned misunderstanding until McCann had dropped the hand and stumbled away in a huff.

Staring at the unsteady figure weaving into the darkness, Samuel had seethed at the ungodliness and the disgusting suggestions of the so-called man. He raised his hand to wipe it on his jacket. He then realised he was still clutching the list his wife set on the table before leaving for her night shift at the steam laundry. The scrap was a squishy lump, compacted by McCann's sweat and pressure. Carefully pulling it apart, Samuel could only make out the last line. "biscuits for Rev. Simons visit Sunday."

The next morning, a very hungover McCann had been unaware he had even spoken to Samuel at the market. From that encounter on, the stevedore prayed for an opportunity to return the contempt with interest. Now, four months later, Samuel watched the little man run along the fir planks, fleeing the darkness of guilty conscious. How true the Proverbs were; the wicked do indeed flee when no man pursueth. He didn't know what personal demons plagued McCann, but it was clear they were at work. At one point in his haste, the pilot nearly slipped off into the mud. Samuel was a little ashamed to think he would have enjoyed seeing that. Just a little.

As he admitted to himself "no, not even a little ashamed," two grimy brown boys, perhaps seven and nine years old, emerged from the muddy lane beside the hotel. One cradled half a dozen wrinkled apples, the other a handful of discarded sausage ends wrapped in a wilted cabbage leaf, obviously scavenged from the hotel's refuse pile. When they saw Samuel eyeing them, the younger seemed fearful he might seize their finds. The older only looked defiant.

Samuel spoke to them in the Language to ask the Indian Questions--those two things whose importance consistently escaped the understanding of Whites, be they American or English or even French. Once the boys told him where they were from and who they were related to, he recounted his own village and family. He was pretty sure they were the children of his wife's cousin's late half-brother. If they were indeed part of that family, these two would refuse to be taken in by anyone, regardless of their circumstances. Proud, too proud. He handed the older boy the coin from McCann. "Buy something to eat. Be careful. And do not lose touch with your people."

He would have done the same even if there was no connection and they were any other of the multitude of colours God made children. Christian charity trumped the need for such a paltry contribution to the church coffers. Pastor Simeon said over and over that Christ lives first in the heart, then in the walls of a church.

"You know the Indian Gospel Church on Pine Street? We share a meal together after Friday evening service. You are always welcome."

He was gratified when the older boy raised his hands in the traditional gesture of thanks, now mostly seen only among old folks. The boys crossed the road, then disappeared between two stables. Samuel turned in the opposite direction, making his way among outbuildings and open sheds to reach the Brickley Air loading platform.

The work gang shouted greetings to their returning foreman. They had been among the crowds of men who pulled the Daphne to the engine shed. Unlike many other workers in the city, the Brickley dockers--red, white, and black (the Asiatic Exclusion League having ensured no Celestials were on the payroll)--were still expected to arrive at six the next morning for a regular twelve-hour shift.

Just after lunch, an office boy showed up as the gang began to empty the freighter from Denver. He called out, "Boss man wants to talk now, Mr. Luke." Samuel told his crew to finish offloading, then move the accumulation of empty pallets to an adjacent shed. He then followed the messenger to the hanger office.

The senior clerk led him upstairs, making his disdain for the platform boss quite clear. He opened the door, impatiently gesturing for Samuel to enter, then closed it a bit too firmly behind him. Arthur Brickley stood at the window, smouldering cigar in hand, staring morosely across the sodden expanse at a pair of tethered airships belonging to a competitor. Beyond them, Union Bay was just visible through the clinging mist. As he had done at the beginning of the shift that morning, he moved straight to business.

"Sam, what the hell. I hear tell McCann boarded the Los Angeles nooner. That would have been after you delivered my message. Killip's bean counters are beside themselves trying to wrap up accounts for my shareholder's meeting. Did you tell McCann we needed to square away the back pay owed him?"

"Yes, sir, Mr Brickley. I tracked him to the Caravan Hotel. They wouldn't let me in or pass a message to the bar.

So I waited until he came out. I told him right as soon as he was out the door. But he wasn't too sober, sir. After I had given him your message, he looked kind of funny, then just turned and headed off towards the terminal."

Brickley shrugged as he drew on the cigar. "Well, he did a hell of a job handling the Daphne yesterday. No reason why he should run off--none that I know of. But pilots are a dime a dozen, and most are birdshit-in-the-eye crazy. Killip is just gonna have to make something up. Don't matter." He drew on the cigar. "Best get on back to the loading bay. The Amanda will be in early from Salt Lake City. Your crew will be working late today. I'll have sandwiches sent around."

As Samuel turned away, Brickley held up a hand. "Hold up, Sam." He pulled a quarter-eagle gold piece from a vest pocket. "Here's a little something for your trouble. I imagine you'll put it to that nice church you folks got going. Your business if you spend it elsewhere."

The stevedore saw the faint smile that did not reach the man's eyes. Still holding firmly on to the coin, Brickley asked, "You sure McCann understood what I wanted? Never knowed a man to leave town to avoid his wages." The Brick eased his hold so Samuel could take the coin.

"Thank you, sir. My boys appreciate you thinking of them. This money will for sure go to Reverend Simeon's lodging. And yes, sir, I told Mr. McCann each and every word you said, sir."

Just not in the same order the Brick had uttered them. Accounts settled.

THE END

Zoe Duff

Zoe lives in Victoria, Canada with her partners, regularly visiting with her eight children and five grandchildren, and enjoys the inspirational company of the Eclectic Writers' Boot Camp group, which she facilitates. She has published eleven books for adults and children. Zoe's short stories, *The Campout* and *Zest for Life* are featured in the *Anthology for a Green Planet* (Filidh 2014); and her short stories, *The Lady and the Adventurer* and *Multi-faceted Love* are featured in The Unvalentine Anthology (Filidh 2015).

Do It Until You Get it Right was originally written as an exercise in her writer's group sessions and fine- tuned for this publication. *Aftermath* was written specifically for this collection

See more from Zoe @ https://www.zoe-duff-author.com or on Twitter @polychicbc

Do It Until You Get It Right

It was a bit crisp for autumn, and Jake could hear the leaves crunching under his feet as he walked. It had been a dreary day, and evening had fallen very quickly. The road was lined with darkened houses on one side and a thick woods on the other. He could feel animal eyes on him and remembered both cougar and bear sighting in recent news items. The hair stood up on the back of his neck, and he wished for more street lamps. A howl to his left and deep inside the woods triggered memories of various werewolf movies. Jake sped up his pace and was fair running down the road when three men dressed in baggy low-riding jeans, hoodies, and ball caps stepped out of the woods in front of him.

"Yer such a pussy, man!"

"Yeah, Jake–scared much?!"

They all laughed and punched each other in congratulations of their mutually keen wit. Jake wasn't sure he was relieved by their presence. He slowed his pace to a stroll as he approached the men. Richard, Braden, and Carl. Jake knew them from school, but avoided doing much with them because they were drifting on the edge of trouble and he was intent on a hockey scholarship.

"What are you bozos doing out here?"

"Some dude looking for dope invited us to a party."

"Yeah, we bring the weed, and he brings the girls."

"In Surrey? Are you crazy?" Jakes' grandmother lived several streets over, and he had to come to this part of Vancouver to visit her, but otherwise, this was an area for Vietnamese and Indian gangs to fight it out lately and most certainly not a place for white wannabe drug dealers to hang out.

"Whatever, man."

"Loser got the address wrong, and we couldn't find the place." Richard motioned to indicate Carl's notetaking inadequacies.

"Let's hope there isn't some carload of assholes out looking for some white dumbasses," said Jake.

He resumed his stroll to King Edward Boulevard and the Scott Road Skytrain station. They grumbled, but they followed him. Reaching the corner of 120th and King Edward, Jake paused for them to catch up and visually gauged the distance to the Skytrain station and the flow of traffic, deciding that jaywalking wasn't worth it. He turned to walk to the Scott Road intersection crosswalk, and a midnight blue Mitsubishi Lancer pulled up on the sidewalk blocking his path. Two Asian men got out and approached them.

"Shouldn't you boys be home with your Mommies?"

"Just on our way there now," said Jake.

"What are you doing around here?"

"Looking for a party but didn't find it," said Richard.

Jake glared at him.

"Ohhhh… so you white boys are looking for some sweet Asian pooosie?"

Braden and Carl laughed and punched each other. Jake sighed. Richard said, "Well, I think the guy who invited us was from India but not sure about the girls."

All of the men in the car got out. Jake had sidled around the car and was able to slowly back away unnoticed. Then the men in the car collectively continued the conversation with the three boys using punches and fists for clarity. While they were distracted with that, Jake was able to run for the Skytrain station. He bolted up the stairs to the waiting area, tripping once on the stairs and falling hard on his butt. Gasping for breath, he looked out the window to the road below. The men from the car had realised that he had run off, and several were running toward the station. Just then a train came, and he jumped on it.

Throwing himself into a seat, he held his head in this hands and sobbed. He had tried very hard to stay out of situations like that all through school, and yet here he was in this mess. He pulled out his phone to call 911 and get some help for his friends. His phone app was playing a video. Jake thought he must have hit the phone in his fall and butt-dialled the app to play. He was about to shut it off and make his phone call, when he noticed that it was a video of Carl getting up off the pavement and going to Richard to help him. Braden was lying on the pavement unconscious. There was lots of blood around, and there were angry voices in the background. The men were yelling about Jake and how to find him. Jake pushed stop on the video and then rewound it to the beginning. He pushed the play icon.

"You are such a good boy to come and take care of your old Gramma," said Mrs. Wiebe.

"But you are my favourite Saturday night date, Gramma," said Jake, picking up dishes from the dinner table and going into the kitchen. Jake placed the dishes on the counter and looked out the kitchen window. The sun was setting, and he was confused. Two seconds ago he'd been on the Skytrain watching that video. Rewind. Had he rewound his day too?

"You don't need to do the dishes, Jakey. I'd rather we spent our time chatting."

"Okay, Gramma. Did you want some more tea?"

"Yes, dear, and grab yourself a slice of that pie on the counter."

"Gramma, would you mind if I stayed overnight tonight?"

"Not at all. The guest room is always ready for you. I thought you had practice early tomorrow, though."

"I just need more Gramma time than usual. I can miss a practice session."

Jake thought he might avoid the whole confrontation with the Asian gang members and keep himself safe. He thought about his friends and decided that they were on their own. Maybe if he hadn't made them walk faster those guys in the car wouldn't have found them. Cutting himself a bigger slice of pie this time, he took it and his grandmother's cup of tea into the living room.

The next morning, social media was flooded with the story that three guys from North Vancouver had been killed in a drive-by shooting at a house in Surrey. Apparently, they had been at a party and gotten in the middle of a gang dispute. No names were released.

"I guess they found the place after all," thought Jake.

He looked at his phone's video app and searched for the last video viewed. This time, the video showed the shooting. Jake heard his Gramma calling that breakfast was ready. He dressed and went down to join her, but his heart was heavy.

"You look worried. Is everything okay?"

"Gramma, if you could do something that might save someone's life, but might also put you at risk, would you do it?"

"What kind of risk?"

"Life and death."

"Save a life and risk your own?"

"Yeah."

"Hmm. Often that isn't a choice. Either you help, or you don't. Emergencies and so on. Most people don't regret the helping, but I'm not going to advise you to risk your life. I'm selfish, and I want you to be around. Tell me more."

Jake told her his story and showed her the video and the social media. Mrs. Wiebe was appalled. She knew that Surrey had gone downhill over the 40 years that she'd lived there, but this gang violence was terrifying. Jenny Wiebe looked at her grandson and saw his potential and how hard he'd worked for his future. She saw too that his heart was good, and he felt guilty for protecting himself from this very strange situation.

"Hit rewind and take a cab from here... uh last night... and pick them up on your way home."

"Take a cab? To my house? That will cost a fortune."

"Well, I'd be asking them to kick in on it, but check your bank balance. Someone sent you $250 for your birthday." Jenny patted her grandson's hand. "In this version of your life, you didn't know they were in trouble and couldn't have helped. You have no guilt. Leave it be, or take a cab and save them and be safe yourself."

"I think I need to save them."

"That's what I thought you'd say. I wonder, if I push rewind this time, will it let me be 20 years old again?" She winked at him and pushed rewind on his phone.

Jake stood on the road and looked around. It was dark, and the woods were alive with howls and other noises. He shuddered. We didn't rewind far enough. Ahead the three boys stepped out of the woods and called to him. What to do?

Jake approached Richard, Carl, and Braden and said that he knew where there was another party. He turned and walked back to his grandmother's house. The boys followed, joking and laughing. Jake wondered what his grandmother would say when he returned, but it seemed to be the best way to avert disaster.

"So are there lots of chicks at this party?"

Standing out front of his grandmother's house, Jake explained that it wasn't a party like that, but that this was his grandmother's house, and that he was going to call a cab for them all from there. There was stuff on the news about gang violence in the area, and he wanted them to be safe.

"You are such a loser, Jake!" said Richard.

"Yeah, no one is going to shoot us. We aren't gang members," said Braden.

"I'm not going to her house. I don't visit my own Gramma. I hate old people. They smell," said Carl.

Jake thought about telling them about the rewind, but decided that would be worse. He went to the door of his grandmother's house and rang the bell. She came to the door.

"Gramma, I need to call a cab."

"I know, dear. I remember. Unfortunately, we didn't rewind more than a few hours. Youth evades me still."

A car drove by and turned the corner. Jake turned and watched it pass. It was the same blue Lancer with the Asian men in it.

"Fast! Get in the house!" he called to the boys who were laughing and punching each other on the sidewalk.

"Fuck off, Loser!" they responded in unison.

The car drove by again, this time faster with shots blazing from the front and back seat on the passenger side. Jake stepped inside and pulled Jenny with him, but not before she was hit.

Jake pulled out of his phone and selected the phone's video app. The video showed his friends in a heap on the sidewalk. He pushed rewind.

Jake stood looking into his locker. He put his books away and gathered what he needed for homework on the weekend. Putting on his jacket, he looked down the hall to see Richard leaning against his locker and talking on his cell phone. He zipped up his backpack, slung it over a shoulder, and closed his locker.

"Hey Richard, what's up this weekend?"

"Not much. Since when do you care?"

"Oh, I thought maybe we could hang out and scare up a party or something," said Jake, waving to Shelley and Marie. "Hey, girls, you interested in hanging out tomorrow night?"

"Where?" asked Shelley, a pretty brunette with a slight figure. Marie tossed her blonde curls and smiled at Richard, whose eyes were on her cleavage.

"Braden has a rec room and a monster flat screen," said Richard in a mesmerised monotone.

Braden joined the group, punching Richard and breaking Marie's trance-like hold on him.

"I do, but I'm babysitting tonight so no hanging out. You know my mom," said Braden.

"Tomorrow night, dickwad," said Richard, punching him.

Carl and Lily met up with the group, and general discussion about the possibilities for Saturday night ensued. Jake had been so focused on his studies and his hockey practice that he hadn't connected with many people outside of the classroom or the rink. This was an interesting revision to the situation. He wondered if it would be successful.

As he walked home, he listened to them chat and wondered why he hadn't done this before. Eventually, they all went their own directions, but it was very pleasant to have that transition from classroom to home with company. Shelley lived two doors down from him, and he'd never walked home with her before. She was beautiful even when she bit her lip and furrowed her brow. She didn't much like Richard's teasing. She smiled like the sun rising when Jake complimented her, and he'd noticed that she walked closer to him and flirted with him a lot. Well, she blushed and tossed her hair. Mom said that this was flirting. He didn't know much about women or how to respond. Gramma said just to be himself, and that would be charming enough. Gramma was a bit biased, though. Jake wished that his dad was still around so that he could give him tips, but his mom was of the opinion that his dad wouldn't be much use in that department. He must have done something right, Jake thought, as he'd been born.

"Thanks for walking me home, Jake," Shelley was saying. "I can take that bag now."

"Oh. Sure. Here you go." Jake handed her the shopping bag of books. "Do you know where Braden lives, or did you want me to pick you up tomorrow night?"

"Oh. That would be great. I'll get Marie to come here, and we can all go together."

"Sounds great. I'll be here about seven, okay?"

"Give me your phone, and I'll put in my number. Just in case you need it."

"Okay. Do you want mine?"

"Oh. Yes, please." Shelley quickly put her details on his contact list while he did the same on her phone.

"Smile. I want a pic of you on my contact list." Jake smiled for the photo. "Perfect."

"You smile too," he said setting his phone up to take a photo of Shelley.

"Oh!" she said, grinning widely and blushing crimson.

Jake walked home chuckling to himself. Girls were weird. He'd have to ask Gramma if he'd figured out the flirting thing. Oh. Gramma.

Mrs. Wiebe picked up on the first ring. "Hello, Jake! Don't come here for dinner tomorrow night. I have something else to do."

"Oh. Okay. I was just going to ask if I could come over on Sunday after practice instead."

"That would be better. Do you remember why Saturday night is no good?"

"Yes, I'm going to hang out with the guys here instead."

"Oh, thank gawd. That was horrendous. I'm looking at moving into a seniors' complex near you in North Vancouver. I've had enough of Surrey."

"Yes, I'm so sorry that I brought that to your door."

"A good lesson for me: Never mind my youth. I want the full of my old age."

"Those guys didn't trust me or believe that I was thinking of them. I need to work on that friendship and not distance myself so much. Hey, I walked a girl home from school today. I'm going to hang out with her tomorrow night too."

"Maybe we got it right this time, Jake."

Aftermath

Just Down the Road

Distant sounds.

Rumbling of a truck and then its back up alarm.

Crows hurling obscenities at each other or some passerby.

Her eyelashes flutter, and limbs stretch slowly. Soft moans as bruises awaken, new wounds reminding old ones and comparing painful anecdotes.

A chain rattles as she struggles to her feet and shakes off the remnants of sleep. She rummages around looking for a sip of water or morsel of food, sniffing each to determine quality and safety of consumption. Days have blurred into weeks, months, and most likely years, but the one constant was never knowing when there would be food again or clean water. Sissy rationed herself on both of these things just in case.

She crouched in the corner and peed over the hole in the floor boards. The natural light was not sufficient to see it, but she knew roughly where it was, having missed and stepped in the hole many times. Getting one's foot stuck in such a place was a nasty way to learn special logistics. She had learned the delicate balance of squatting in a similar fashion each time.

Sissy wondered if this would be a hose-down day. They used a fire hose to shower her and wash out the piss hole.

Sometimes they gave her a fresh blanket and took away the food dishes to clean as well. Usually, it was the younger man who did that, and he would rub Sissy with a towel. The older man shoved her out into the yard to dry off instead.

The yard was a gravel lot with a small patch of grass surrounded on three sides by eight-foot brick walls, and the fourth side was the big garage where her cage was stored. There were other cages, but they seemed to be empty. She never heard or saw anyone else but the two men.

The lock on the door rattled. She tensed. Every hair stood on end. Every muscle at the ready. Fear making her whole body vibrate.

The door swung wide, and the older man stepped in just far enough to unhook the chain and pull her outside by the metal collar around her neck. Sissy winced and yelped as the metal bit into her wounded flesh again.

The younger man stood outside holding the big fire hose and shooting a steady stream of water at the far wall. The older man unhooked the chain from her collar and shoved her into the stream of water. Sissy closed her eyes and allowed her body to become accustomed to the cold water. She opened her mouth and drank thirstily from the stream. The pressure of the water caused her to stumble backwards into the wall. Well, not quite the wall. This was a softer contact than a brick wall should be.

An arm wrapped around Sissy and she was pulled closer to the softness. The flow of water moved and was now hitting the wall near them instead. Sissy opened her eyes and looked into the face of a woman who was shivering violently enough for both of them.

Loud voices filled the yard.

Angry words and gunshots ricocheted off the walls. Sissy heard the woman sobbing. She felt sobs rise in her throat too, but they passed her teeth as growls. The young man was lying face down on the ground, with a police officer straddling him and applying handcuffs. The older man's feet were sticking out of Sissy's cage. He wasn't moving. Sissy imagined his face in the piss hole and began to giggle.

Hysteria.

A police officer crouched down and asked the woman for her name and other questions, but she only nodded and sobbed. Other police officers wrapped blankets around Sissy and the woman. They were taken out of the yard and through the garage to a waiting ambulance. Sissy saw a big house with many cars and a large field of corn. It was a farm.

Sissy had arrived unconscious on the bad day so long ago and had never seen anything beyond the garage and yard. She looked around as the paramedics tended her wounds. She recognised the road and remembered her farm. Home. Sissy began to cry, her tears welling up from deep down inside where the fear and pain had been stuffed. The buried emotions flowed out of her in an endless stream and with a power that made the fire hose pale in comparison.

The woman pulled her close, and they shared a release that only those who experience such trauma can understand. A release that wakes you in the night with memories unwrapping like putrid onion skin, peeling off your deepest thoughts. A release that paralyses you when a brief moment triggers recollections. It feels like an open wound. It never goes away.

The younger man was being questioned. The older man went by in a body bag on a stretcher and was loaded into the ambulance. Police were everywhere, exploring the house and garage. Sissy sat on the front porch of the house whining softly and sipping from a cup of water. The woman had been driven home by a police officer. Another officer remained with Sissy. They didn't know where she "belonged." She got up, walked to the garden, squatted and peed. She would not get in a car. She would not be in anything again.

One of the police officers stopped and watched Sissy thoughtfully. Clearly, this one had been mistreated for a long time and would have some difficulty recovering. The officer walked over to Sissy and asked if she were hungry. Sissy cowered. The question "Hungry?" was always followed by a beating. Sissy hung her head and looked up through her eyelashes at this new man, waiting for the first punch.

A car pulled up near the porch, and an old woman got out with measured movements. The driver of the car got out and came around to assist her. He motioned to the house, and the two walked up the steps to the porch and into the house. The old woman leant heavily on the driver for support. A police officer greeted them and then came back out calling for Sissy to come into the house.

The officer tried to bring Sissy into the house but she crawled into a fetal position and sobbed. The old woman sat at the kitchen table, and the driver sat with her. Sissy allowed herself to be brought to the porch window that looked in on the kitchen. The old woman was familiar. She smelled of lavender and oatmeal cookies. Sissy remembered the smell. She vibrated with fear and excitement. Could this be "belong"?

Shaking with fear and exhaustion, Sissy slowly crawled in the window and sat on the floor beside the old woman's chair. She looked up with sad, hopeful eyes. The old woman placed a hand on Sissy's head and stroked the matted hair. Her grandchild was unrecognisable for the most part. So much time had passed. Long matted hair, and grubby dress aside. Here was a young adult! The child had been six years old when he disappeared. The police had run his DNA through their system. She didn't need that, though. One look at those eyes. This was Brian, her grandson.

The janitor at his elementary school had taken a shine to him because all the kids teased him and called him "sissy". He was a delicate child, for sure, but children could be cruel. It turns out the janitor had been nastier. Her heart ached for what Brian had been through. What the police could surmise of it, at least. She could see that they didn't know the half of it. She turned in her chair and opened her arms. Sissy leapt into her embrace.

"Belong."

The driver spoke softly to the old woman about counselling and recovery. She nodded, wiping tears from her cheeks. Sissy saw the tears and patted her grandmother's arm as the other woman had done earlier. She knew somehow that this was good and that she was safe.

She closed her eyes and listened to the sound of the old woman's heart beating.

"Belong."

About Filidh Publishing Authors

We are a group of authors who meet regularly to hone our skills in writing, publishing, marketing and networking.

Filidh Publishing facilitates the Eclectic Writers Boot Camp group and hosts Double Dog Dare Open Mic events for unpublished authors to step up to the mic and read their work aloud for the positive feedback of applause. Published authors are invited to read from their works, sell copies, and build a fan base for that dream career of being a full-time author.

This is the third annual anthology of short stories produced by Filidh Publishing. Most authors in this book have stood at the open mic and dared to tell their stories. We hope to inspire you to dare to follow your dreams. We Double Dog Dare you!!

For event notices watch:

On Facebook @FilidhPublishing , on Twitter @filidhbooks, And at https://filidhbooks.com

www.ingramcontent.com/pod-product-compliance
Lightning Source LLC
Chambersburg PA
CBHW020323260626
47156CB00004B/1347